Dog Day Wedding

Rich Amooi

Dog Day Wedding

**GET UPDATES ON
NEW RELEASES & EXCLUSIVE DEALS!**
Sign up for Rich's newsletter at:
http://www.richamooi.com/newsletter

To the love of my life.

My honeybunch.

I love you more today than yesterday.

But not as much as tomorrow.

Chapter One

"Somebody kill me," muttered Giovanni Roma, fiddling with his cufflinks.

All Giovanni wanted was a nice, simple wedding at a country club or winery. He wasn't picky. His dream was to be married and to have a wonderful family with kids. That's all.

The house with the white picket fence? Not even necessary.

Why would a white fence bring you happiness anyway? It's just wood. Painted.

Giovanni tried to keep his thoughts positive, but it wasn't easy. His fiancée had insisted on a traditional church ceremony. He wasn't going to argue. Anything to make Patricia happy.

But Patricia had forgotten one tiny little detail though. The part where she was supposed to show up.

"Where is she?" whispered Giovanni.

He stared at the empty doorway of the church, along with the guests.

"Don't worry, she's coming," said Danny Castro, slapping his best friend on the back. "Relax."

Giovanni wiped the sweat from his forehead and blew out

a deep breath. "Relax. Right."

All the Valium in the world wouldn't be able to relax him.

The organist continued to play "Canon in D" for the bride's entrance.

Danny smacked Giovanni on the arm with the back of his hand. "Maybe she got caught up in traffic behind the circus and an elephant got loose or something."

Here we go.

"Come on," said Stevie Marino, the other best man. "That's not realistic at all. She's probably putting crop circles in her parents' wheat field. To keep out the aliens."

"A big sale at Macy's?" said Danny, raising his eyebrows and looking for approval.

Stevie held up a finger. "She got busted at the airport for being a drug mule!"

The priest reached over and covered the microphone with his hand. "Please."

Stevie winced. "Forgive me, Father, for I have sinned."

Giovanni glanced over at his two best friends. The guys looked sharp in their matching black tuxedos and red ties. As crazy as they drove him, they meant well. They were just trying to distract him from the current situation at hand. But nothing was going to make him laugh. His bride-to-be was currently a no-show.

What if something bad had happened to Patricia?

"Maybe we should call her," said Giovanni.

The priest gave Giovanni a reassuring smile. "These things

always seem to run off schedule. Give it a few more minutes."

"Okay."

Giovanni's gaze traveled around the dome of the cathedral, admiring the saints portrayed on each of the colorful stained glass windows. His eyes stopped on St. Francis of Assisi.

The priest pointed to the window. "Do you know the story of St. Francis?"

Giovanni turned to the priest. "No."

"You may find it particularly fascinating—his original name was Giovanni."

"No way!" said Danny.

The priest nodded. "His mother gave birth to him while the father was away on a trip to France. She named him Giovanni. When the father returned he didn't like the name she gave him, so he changed it."

Stevie squeezed Giovanni's arm. "I like your name."

"Me too," said Danny. "And no matter what happens here today, I want you to know you're the nicest guy I've ever known."

Giovanni smiled. He couldn't ask for better friends.

"Patricia will be coming through that door any second," said Danny. "I guarantee it."

Giovanni stared at the entry of the church. The guests' whispers were getting louder.

Danny pointed to the organist. "While we're waiting, did

you know Pachelbel's 'Canon in D' was composed almost four hundred years ago?"

Stevie sighed. "Myself, along with the majority of the other good-looking, upstanding citizens of this country, don't give a flying steamy turd about Pocket Ball."

"Pachelbel."

"Him too."

Danny ignored him. "His compositions were forgotten for centuries."

"I guarantee you it'll take me a lot less time to forget."

The song ended and the church attendants closed the doors. A few seconds later the organist started the processional again and they reopened the doors.

"Bingo," said Stevie, watching the entry and spotting a woman.

A large woman appeared in the doorway wearing a bright yellow dress and an oversized hat loaded with bird feathers.

Stevie frowned. "Maybe not."

The woman was like a deer in headlights. Everyone in the church stared at her.

"Oh my," she said and quickly sat in the last row.

The doors closed again and the music stopped.

Giovanni rubbed the back of his neck. "Unbelievable."

A minute later the music started up again and the church attendants swung open the doors for the third time, revealing a golden retriever.

A man jumped up from one of the seats and yelled.

"Cinnamon! How did you get out of the car?" He squeezed by the guests in his row one by one. "Excuse me. Pardon me. Oops, so sorry."

He snagged Cinnamon by the collar and led him toward the doors, but not before the dog had a chance to lift his leg and pee on the side of one of the pews. The man dragged the dog outside and the doors closed behind him.

Giovanni adjusted the lapel on his tuxedo jacket. "Welcome to Ringling Brothers."

"Shit," said Stevie. "This is starting to really suck."

The priest cleared his throat and pointed to the microphone with his index finger.

"Whoops. Forgive me, Father, for I have sinned again. And hey, while you're at it, can you forgive me for the rest of the week? I really don't have a good feeling about it."

"You can't cover yourself for the future."

"Why not?"

"Asking for forgiveness only covers the past."

"I have to keep asking for forgiveness over and over again?"

The priest nodded.

Stevie let out a loud breath. "That's very time consuming."

The priest turned to Giovanni. "You know, I have another wedding directly after this one. I can only give her a few more minutes. Then we'll have to, uh—reschedule."

Giovanni held out his hand to Stevie. "Give me your phone. I'm going to call Patricia."

Stevie pulled the cell phone from his pocket and handed it to Giovanni.

"Wait a minute," said Danny. He scratched the side of his face and looked around the church. "I just realized something…it's not just Patricia who's missing. We don't have any bridesmaids here either. Or Patricia's parents."

"Uh oh," said Stevie. "I'm getting a *serious* déjà vu."

Unbelievable.

It was much worse. Giovanni had thought maybe something terrible had happened to Patricia. If that was the case, a friend or family member would have rushed to tell him.

But that wasn't the case at all. Giovanni didn't like that feeling in his gut.

He was going to get jilted at the altar.

Again.

Shit.

How could he have missed that? Danny was right. There were two empty spots in the front row where Patricia's parents should have been sitting.

What did Giovanni do to deserve this? He was a decent person. He donated blood every year. He always bought Girl Scout cookies when neighbor kids came knocking on the door. He vividly remembered helping a little old lady cross the street not that long ago. He had a very successful guitar-making business and even donated guitars every year to underprivileged youths. Was the person in charge of karma on vacation? It wasn't fair.

In the back of his mind he wondered if today's disaster was his mother's fault again. *She* was the cause of the runaway bride at his first almost-wedding. Well, she technically wasn't really a runaway bride—more like a didn't-even-bother-to-show-up bride.

Like the one today.

Giovanni stared at his mother, Eleonora Roma, sitting in the front row next to his father, Alfonso. She was staring right back at him with her inquisitive round brown eyes, not even blinking.

She wasn't a happy camper.

Eleonora stood up and brushed off her elegant cream-colored dress and approached the front.

"Incoming," warned Stevie.

"Wonderful," mumbled Giovanni.

Eleonora was unpredictable and had a tendency to make a scene. She obviously knew there was a problem, but Giovanni was not in the mood to discuss it with his mom. Maybe he could compliment her on her new hairdo to distract her. Her short, curly golden-gray hair was more a light ash blond now in a full fringe style with volume and body. He could tell her it was very flattering to her round face, making her look a lot younger than sixty.

Right.

Who was he kidding? She would spot Giovanni's insincere compliment a mile away. He had a much better idea. Better to get out of there. Now.

Eleonora opened her mouth to speak, but Giovanni stopped her before she could say a word.

"I need to use the bathroom," he lied. "Be right back."

Giovanni slid right by his mother and headed to the exit. Two hundred eyes followed him as he walked down the aisle toward the door. Danny and Stevie would take care of the inquiring guests and sort things out. He felt guilty, but he just didn't want to deal with it.

Not this time.

*****

Giovanni got in his car in the church parking lot and quickly pulled his cell phone from the center compartment. Maybe Patricia had left him a message.

Nope. Nothing.

Why hadn't she at least called to explain things? To let him know why she decided not to show up?

Giovanni slid the phone into his tuxedo jacket pocket. He got on the road and drove through Los Gatos—a small, wealthy Silicon Valley town with a population pushing thirty thousand. After a few cars honked at him, he pulled over and erased "Just Married" from the back window of the car with his hand. He wiped his hand on the side of his tuxedo pants, got back in the car, and drove.

It was one of the most beautiful days of the summer, but

he wished he were somewhere else. Anywhere but here. He sat at a red light deep in thought. He looked down at his tuxedo and swallowed hard. His love life was a disaster.

He needed a distraction. Anything at all, really.

An older woman with tall hair interrupted his thoughts.

"Help!" she screamed, pointing to the other side of the street. "Someone please grab my dog!"

Giovanni cranked his head around and saw a small dog—a Yorkie—darting in and out from between the cars. The dog turned and ran in the direction of Giovanni's car, disappearing underneath it. Giovanni put the car in park, opened the door, and jumped out. He looked under the car for the dog. Nothing.

Where did it go?

The woman screamed again and pointed at a FedEx truck about a hundred feet away. It was headed straight for the dog who was now in the middle of the street licking himself. Thoughts of the dog being hit prompted Giovanni to jump in front of the truck.

He threw his arms up in the air. "Stop!"

The FedEx driver slammed on the brakes, the tires skidded, and the truck stopped a foot from Giovanni. He let out a deep breath and gave a thumbs-up to the driver for his quick reflexes. Giovanni ran by his car, slammed the door shut, and hopped on the sidewalk to chase the dog.

A man in a silver Land Rover honked his horn and rolled down his window. "Hey! You can't leave your car there!"

Giovanni waved to the man and continued his pursuit of the dog. "Sorry! I'll be right back!"

When he was a little boy Giovanni had lost a dog and it was a very traumatic experience. He didn't know the old lady, but he knew she was distressed and was determined to catch the dog for her.

"Here boy!" yelled Giovanni, picking up speed.

The dog didn't respond to his yell.

"Here girl!"

The dog continued down the sidewalk past the Apple Store and Andale Taqueria—its cute little butt shaking back and forth. It had a pink collar that jingled with every step.

Pink collar. Definitely a girl.

Giovanni wracked his brain for female dog names.

"Fifi!"

Nothing.

"Smooches!"

Nope.

"Rosebud!"

She kept running through the intersection toward Town Plaza Park.

"Muffin! Pookie!"

Not even close.

"Precious!"

The dog suddenly stopped in the park under the redwoods trees, across from the post office. She turned to look back at Giovanni.

Nobody was more surprised than the out-of-breath man in the tuxedo.

She was a small dog, but long and lean. Her shiny gray and tan hair looked silky and fine. It was neatly trimmed short. Her tail was barely higher than her body.

The dog moved closer to sniff Giovanni's pant legs.

He reached down to scratch her on the head. "You're a cute little thing. Fast too. Is that really your name? Precious?"

After a couple of scratches between her ears the dog rolled over on her back on the grass, asking for more. Giovanni obliged—rubbing her belly. He rotated the collar around so he could read the tag.

Precious.

Giovanni grinned. "Hello, Precious. What are you doing running all over the place? Did you know your mommy is worried about you?"

She barked as if she was answering his question.

Giovanni laughed. "That's not safe what you did, you know?"

She barked again.

"Do you want to get hurt? Of course you don't!"

Giovanni realized he was talking in a doggy voice and looked around to see if anyone noticed.

Nobody. Good.

He rubbed her belly a few more times and picked her up. He held her close to his chest as he walked back down North Santa Cruz Avenue to find the owner.

Precious reached up and licked Giovanni on the chin.

Giovanni laughed again. "You getting frisky with me?"

"Arf!"

She licked him on the chin again and appeared to be smiling, her caramel sparkling eyes on him.

Giovanni approached the owner and smiled, handing her the dog.

"Precious!" said the old woman. She had a smile that covered her entire face. "You're such a bad girl. I was worried sick." She hugged the dog and kissed her on top of the head.

"Well, the good thing is she's okay," said Giovanni.

The tiny woman smiled again. "Thank you, young man. What's your name?"

"Giovanni."

She lit up. "An Italian boy."

He nodded.

"I'm Beatrice. My late husband was Italian. He looked exactly like Luciano Pavarotti but bigger."

"Bigger than Pavarotti?"

Beatrice waved off Giovanni's question with her hand. "I didn't care about that. I just wanted someone who kissed well and *that* he did!"

"Lucky you."

"Yes! Lucky me! We had a passionate love affair and in the bedroom he would—"

"Oh God!" yelled Giovanni, startling the woman.

Too much information.

Especially coming from a stranger who could be in her late seventies.

Giovanni pretended to look at his watch. Hopefully she didn't notice he wasn't wearing one.

"I need to get going," he said.

He didn't want to sound rude.

The woman was nice and he was happy Precious was safe, but Giovanni just wanted to go home and sulk. Precious started whining and tried to squirm out of Beatrice's arms toward Giovanni.

He reached out and petted her again. "You take care, Precious. And quit running out into the street."

"You must be someone very special. Precious has never been a big fan of the male species."

Species?

"Before you go, come here."

Giovanni had no idea what she meant. He was already *there.* Maybe she wanted to hug him to say thanks. His focus went to her thin, gravity-defying hair. He knew the color had to be fake, but how the heck did she make it stand up straight like that? It looked stiff and rough and didn't budge an inch when the breeze hit it. It was like the world's largest scouring pad.

He had the sudden urge to wash dishes.

Beatrice grabbed Giovanni by the side of the head with her free hand and before he could react, she pulled him down for a kiss. Not a kiss on the cheek either. Precious joined in on the action and licked his face like he'd just rubbed in some steak juice. He was surprised how much effort he needed to pry the woman from his lips.

Giovanni pulled away and wiped his mouth instinctively. He forced a smile. "That really wasn't necessary."

"I think it was. I can't thank you enough. In fact, give me your phone number."

"Pardon me?"

Beatrice pulled out her cell phone and handed it to Giovanni. "Your number, what is it? Just type it in there."

He raised his gaze to meet hers. "My number? For what?" He crinkled his nose and stared at her phone.

"Are you constipated?" she asked.

"No, I'm fine."

"Then punch in the numbers!"

She certainly was a forceful woman, kind of like Giovanni's mom. No. That wasn't fair. His mom was in a category all by herself. This woman wasn't like his mother at all. Beatrice was just very…outgoing. There was a big difference.

Giovanni hesitated but then typed in his number.

"Now press send," said Beatrice.

He looked up at her again.

"Do it."

He pressed send and a few seconds later the phone in his jacket pocket rang. He pulled the phone out and stared at it.

14

Beatrice plucked the phone from his hand and disconnected the call. "Perfect! Now I have your number! I'll be in touch. Thanks again. You're a doll."

She reached up and pulled him down by the neck again and kissed him on the lips.

Again.

Then she smiled and walked away.

Giovanni turned and spotted a female police officer in front of his car.

Writing him a ticket.

He ran up the street toward the cop and waved his hand in the air at her. "Hey, hey, I'm right here. No need for that —I was just leaving."

The most beautiful brown eyes Giovanni had ever seen turned around to greet him and then checked him out from head to toe.

"Nice tux," the cop said.

"Oh…" He looked down at his tux. "Thank you." He forgot he was actually wearing one and that it was his wedding day. Precious proved to be a wonderful distraction. Or maybe it was the cop's big eyes framed by long dark eyelashes.

Giovanni waited for her to say something else, but she turned her attention back to writing the ticket. She was an attractive woman with a pretty face and light brown hair up in a bun. Her olive complexion was smooth and she didn't seem to wear any makeup at all.

She almost didn't seem like a real cop to him. He had the idea that female cops were more intimidating, like in the movies. She was petite and appeared delicate—didn't seem that tough at all. No doubt she used that to her advantage. She could probably kick Giovanni's ass with her pinkie.

Giovanni pointed to her ticket pad. "You don't really need to do that, do you?"

She stopped writing and looked up. "You abandoned your car on the street. Safety hazard."

"I was just trying to help a woman. I saved a dog! That's not against the law, is it?"

"Not at all. But leaving your car *here* is. People die."

Giovanni let out a nervous chuckle. "From stationary cars?"

"Someone can swerve to avoid your car and run over an innocent child walking home from school."

"It's Saturday."

"Okay…walking home from Saturday school."

Was she serious? Was there such a thing?

"Look," said Giovanni. "I didn't want to play the sympathy card, but it looks like I have no other choice. I'm having a horrible day. *Horrible.* I was supposed to get married today and my fiancée never showed up. I was on my way home from the church and heard a woman cry for help. So that's what I was doing, just trying to help her. Her dog got loose." Giovanni sighed. "I thought women were supposed to be fond of heroes."

The cop laughed and ended it with a snort. "You think you're a hero?"

"Yeah! Why not? I rescued her dog. Look, I know it's not worthy of a medal of honor or anything like that. But I'm just asking you to give me a break today. That's all. Please."

The cop studied Giovanni for a few moments. "You rescued the dog?"

"Yes! Then the woman thanked me by kissing me on the lips."

She pointed to Giovanni's face. "I can see that."

Giovanni wiped his mouth and saw the lipstick on his fingers. "It's not what you think. She must have been two hundred years old. Call me picky, but I prefer my women to be around a hundred and seventy years younger."

The officer snorted again.

She stared at Giovanni for a moment, her smile fading. "You really got left at the altar?"

He nodded.

"Sorry to hear that." She stared at the ticket pad momentarily and closed it. "Okay. Verbal warning. Watch where you leave your car, okay? You're free to go."

"Thank you! Can I hug you?"

"No."

"Okay, not a problem. But just know that something good's going to happen to you for your kindness. I'm sure of it."

"I can't wait." She gave him a wide smile that pulled his

attention back to her natural pink lips and her perfectly aligned teeth. She could sell millions of dollars of toothpaste by flashing those pearly whites.

Giovanni got back in his car and smiled. There were at least two positive things that happened today. One, he saved Precious. And two, there was that kind and pretty cop who let him off the hook. He was certain she was going to give him the ticket but she surprised the hell out of him.

Hopefully there wouldn't be any more surprises today.

Chapter Two

Giovanni walked into his home and closed the door behind him. It was a modest place; three bedrooms, two baths. He even had a shop in the backyard where he built his guitars. He had only owned the house for two years and he felt very comfortable there. Patricia liked the place as well. She had practically moved in—spending so much time there lately. Giovanni even had cleared some space in his dresser and closet so she could keep some of her things there. But that was over.

Time to move on.

He took a deep breath and began to remove his bow tie, dropping it on the hardwood floor in the entryway. He slid off his tuxedo jacket, shirt, shoes, pants, and socks and dropped them all on the floor as well.

He stood there in his underwear, deep in thought, staring at the photo on the wall of him and Patricia dining at a restaurant on her birthday. He wasn't smiling in the photo.

Maybe that was a sign.

Or maybe that was right after he got the bill. She certainly liked to spend his money. But it didn't matter anymore. Right now he was trying to figure out if he was more pissed off, disappointed, or hurt.

Pissed off. Definitely.

He ground his teeth and went out to the side yard, grabbing the garbage can to wheel it inside the house. The faster he could move on and get some closure, the better.

"Giovanni!" said his seventy-five year old Italian neighbor, Federico DeMarco. "Buona sera!"

Giovanni stopped in his tracks and turned around slowly. Federico stood there with a big smile on his face, as usual. He always looked so elegant and old-fashioned in his plaid pants and pressed shirts. He was losing some of the solid-white hair in the front, but liked to keep it longer in the back—like many of the older Italian guys.

Federico was a good guy, but Giovanni preferred to talk with the man when he was fully clothed.

Giovanni moved behind the garbage can and forced a smile. "Hi Federico."

"You don't have to be embarrassed," said Federico. He pointed to Giovanni's underwear. "You think you are the first person to forget to put on pants before leaving the house? Ha! When Olive was alive, let me tell you—"

"Excuse me, Federico!" Giovanni entered the house and shut the door behind him. Federico was possibly the nicest guy he knew, but he just wasn't in the mood to talk to him right now. Or anyone, for that matter. He would explain to Federico what happened to him another time and apologize for being rude.

Giovanni rolled the garbage can into the family room and pulled the one solo picture frame he had of the two of them, dumping it in the garbage can. That should have been a clue; they only had one happy photo together. He didn't react to the sound of broken glass.

He headed to the bathroom next, opening up the medicine cabinet. He corralled the female beauty products and threw them in the trash. He pulled the pink toothbrush from the holder, perfume and lotion bottles from the counter, a package of tampons from under the sink, and shampoos and conditioners from the shower. They all went in the trash.

One more stop.

Giovanni rolled the garbage can toward the dresser in the bedroom, bumping into the wall and the bed along the way. He opened up the top of the dresser and pulled out women's panties, bras, and clothes, dumping them in the trash. He slid open the closet door and yanked a few clothes from hangers, high-heeled shoes from the hanging shoe holder, and expensive designer purses from the shelf.

They all went in the trash.

Giovanni rolled the receptacle back toward the side door of the house and slowly opened it, checking to see if Federico was still there. Satisfied the coast was clear, he rolled the garbage can outside and stuck it back in its place.

Federico popped back into view from the other side of the fence. "Still can't find those pants?"

Giovanni jumped. "Uh…"

"That reminds me of a story…"

"Not now, Federico. Sorry."

"Of course, of course. I will tell it to you some other time."

Giovanni shut the door behind him and grabbed a beer from the fridge. After the first sip he sat on the couch. The doorbell rang. He stared at the door but didn't move. He took another sip of his beer as the doorbell continued to ring in rapid succession. Then it suddenly stopped. Giovanni listened, wondering if the ringing was going to return. No. He was convinced they were gone.

"Thank God."

The ringing started again. He had a sudden thought.

Was it Patricia?

His heart rate sped up with the thought. She had a key, but maybe she had left it at her place. What would he say to her? He jumped up and opened the door.

Stevie and Danny stood there in their tuxes. They still looked sharp, but he was in no mood to talk.

Danny was the tallest of the three friends, skinnier, with dark straight hair, cut in layers to his shoulders. His hazel eyes and pale skin always made people wonder where his family was originally from. Stevie was the shortest. He had dirty blond hair and dark blue eyes, still with the expression of a naughty ten-year-old who was always getting in trouble.

They pushed by Giovanni and walked straight to the kitchen. Giovanni followed.

I just want to be alone.

Stevie grabbed two beers from the fridge and handed one to Danny. He twisted the top off, set it on the counter, and took a sip. "I told you he'd be freaking out like a little girl. Look at him. Half naked and half drunk."

Giovanni took another sip of his beer and went back to the couch. "I'm not drunk yet. And I'm not in the mood, fellas. I need some time to reflect."

Stevie stood in front of Giovanni. "Reflect all you want, but we need to comfort you, Giovanni. I read about it in a used book I found at the Salvation Army. It's called *How to Give People What They Need*. There's also a special chapter on tantric sex."

"I don't need comfort and I most definitely do not need tantric sex."

"Yes, you do."

"These women are walking all over you, Giovanni!" said Danny.

"But no more!" said Stevie. "Consider us like a search party. We're here to help you find your balls."

Giovanni couldn't believe what he was hearing.

Stevie took another sip of his beer and belched. "You need to be more masculine and we're going to help you. That's what friends are for."

Danny smiled. "That was a big hit from Dionne Warwick. 1984."

Stevie jabbed Danny with his finger. "Knock it off."

"What?"

"You know what."

Giovanni pointed toward the door. "Get out."

Danny ignored Giovanni and sat down on the couch next to him. He eyed his underwear. "If it makes you feel more comfortable we can lose our pants."

Giovanni ran his fingers through his hair and sighed. "No. Don't do that. Just leave."

"Not gonna happen," said Stevie. "You are not going through this alone. What just happened to you was some serious shit. You could be mentally fucked up for life. Or even longer."

The front door swung open again and Giovanni's mother, Eleonora, stepped inside. She was still wearing her formal outfit from the wedding and way too much makeup.

She stood there with her hands on her hips. "Why did you leave the church like that?"

Giovanni took a sip of his beer and pretended to read the label on the beer bottle. "I wasn't aware I was supposed to socialize after getting dumped."

Eleonora pointed at Giovanni. "*You* are such a pussy."

Giovanni jerked his head back. "Seriously? You're calling your son a pussy? Whose mother calls her son a pussy?"

Danny raised his hand. "Not all the time, though."

Stevie sighed. "My mom says I'm retarded, but I've proved her wrong on more than a few occasions." He gave a proud nod and took a sip of his beer.

"Please," said Eleonora. "I'm trying to speak to my son here."

Giovanni took another sip of his beer. "We have nothing to talk about."

"You could at least be a man about this. God knows it had to be your fault she left you anyway. What did you do to her?"

"What did *I* do? Nothing!"

Eleonora paced back and forth. "Maybe if you *did* something you wouldn't be in this mess! You know the process."

"Process? What process?"

"You go to school, you get an education, you get your rocks off with a few sluts along the way—"

"Seriously? Who came up with this?"

Eleonora ignored his question. "But then you *realize* at some point that you're supposed to settle down, get married, and have lots of babies. That's how it works! Lots of babies!"

"Oh yeah? Says who?"

"I do! And I want fucking grandchildren!"

"That really surprises me since it's only the thousandth time you told me that! You don't think I want some kids? I thought I was on the right path. I should be married right now!"

"You need to drag your skinny little ass back to her and apologize for whatever you did!"

"I didn't do shit! I've never ever cheated on anybody or

disrespected her in any way. Why do you assume it's my fault, Mom?"

Stevie looked toward the kitchen and then back to Giovanni. "You got any popcorn?"

"Out. Everybody. Now."

The front door opened and in walked Giovanni's dad, Alfonso, a man in his early sixties who looked ten years older. With slumped shoulders and a frown, Giovanni's father slowly dragged his feet towards the living room.

Giovanni pointed to him. "You too, out."

Alfonso squinted his eyes at Eleonora. Then he looked over to Stevie and Danny. Then back to Eleonora. "What did you say to him?"

Eleonora pointed to herself. "Me? Why would you assume I said something?"

"Because I know you."

Stevie turned to Alfonso. "She called Giovanni a pussy."

Eleonora took a step toward Stevie—her nostrils flaring.

Stevie jumped back. "What?"

"Out!" said Giovanni.

Alfonso squeezed his son's shoulder and everyone left without saying another word.

Giovanni grabbed a bottle of tequila from the top of the fridge and got out four shot glasses from the cupboard. He lined up the shot glasses side by side on the kitchen counter and began to pour tequila into each glass. He saw someone do that in a movie once and he thought it was very dramatic.

He placed the bottle on the counter and slammed each

shot, one by one.

What happened was bullshit.

Giovanni knew he was a decent guy—kind, respectful, generous. He didn't deserve what had happened but he needed to find out why it happened twice, to prevent the trifecta. In the meantime there was something he needed to do. He went to the garage to get a can of lighter fluid and a box of matches. He needed closure and he needed it now.

Chapter Three

Natalie DeMarco slipped on an apron over her police uniform and grilled ham for the sandwiches she was about to prepare. She loved cooking in her grandfather's kitchen. Federico had a five-burner stainless steel gas stove and all of the best tools, gadgets, and cookware from Bed Bath & Beyond. It was a chef's paradise.

Federico watched her from the kitchen table. "I'm going to confess something to you right now."

Natalie flipped the ham over in the pan. "I don't believe you."

Federico chuckled. "Let me tell you first! *Then* you can choose whether you want to believe me or not!"

Nono—as Natalie liked to call him—was fun to hang out with. He was known for telling a story or two and sometimes it was not easy figuring out which ones were true. He was the best storyteller she knew.

"Fine. Go for it."

"Your grandmother and I had premarital sex."

"Right!" said Natalie DeMarco, laughing. "Nice try, Nono, but I don't buy it."

"It's true." He got up from the kitchen table and moved

next to her by the stove. "It was practically unheard of in those days, but we couldn't keep our hands off each other!"

"You're just saying that because Nana's not here to confirm it."

Federico grinned and put his hand on her shoulder. "Come here. I want to show you something—then maybe you'll understand."

She pointed the tongs at the ham sizzling in the pan. "I'm preparing your favorite sandwich and you want me to stop so you can show me something? I guess you're not very hungry."

"I am! And that smells fantastico, but this is important. Just one moment, please."

"Okay, just a second." She lifted the pan from the burner and set it aside. After she turned off the gas, she wiped her hands on a kitchen towel and followed Federico to the wall of picture frames in the hallway.

She smiled and pointed. "You put up some new pictures."

"Yes! Look at this one." Federico pointed to a picture of him kissing his wife Olive underneath the Eiffel Tower.

"That's beautiful. What year was that?"

He thought about it for a moment and scratched the side of his face. "During the last century, I'm sure of it."

Natalie laughed and kissed him on the cheek. "Silly."

He chuckled and pointed to a picture of him kissing Olive on a boat. "This one too. Notice what we are doing there?"

She smiled. "*Yes*, Nono. Kissing."

Then he pointed to yet another photo of him kissing Olive on the ski slopes. "And here. Look."

"Okay," said Natalie. "I see the pattern. Kissing is the theme."

"Your grandmother was a kissing machine when she was younger."

Natalie smiled. "Okay, I love the new pictures you put up. But what do I need to understand from all of this?"

Federico put his arm around Natalie's shoulder. "Most couples when they meet are very affectionate. And those who have something very special will continue to be affectionate for the rest of their lives. That was your Nana and me. We had something magical." He hesitated, almost like he didn't want to say it. "I don't ever see you and Jacks kiss at all. This worries me."

Natalie had hoped it wasn't that noticeable. Nono was right; she and Jacks didn't kiss often. It's not like she didn't want to kiss. She loved to kiss! But for some reason her fiancé wasn't as passionate as she was. But he had been very busy and stressed with work lately, and it's hard to be romantic under those conditions.

That's not bad, is it? Opposites attract and can be in healthy relationships!

At least that's what people have said.

"Olive was always on my mind," he continued. "I wanted to spend every waking minute with her. We had a very strong connection and I always wanted to kiss her." He laughed.

"Not as much as she wanted to kiss me! So I ask you, is that how you feel?"

"Well…"

"Marriage shouldn't be rushed into."

"I know, but he said it would be best if we got married before the end of the year." She cleared her throat. "For tax purposes."

Federico frowned.

"Yeah. Not very romantic, but that's the lawyer in him talking." The doorbell rang and Natalie looked toward the door. "He does have a romantic side. He texted me and said he was stopping by just to say hello."

Federico didn't look convinced. "And to eat your famous grilled-ham sandwiches."

"Yeah, that too."

The doorbell rang again.

Natalie forced a smile at Federico.

She opened the door to her fiancé, Jackson Cole—he preferred to be called Jacks. At six-two and two hundred ten pounds, his athletic build made any suit look good. Today was no exception. He was looking mighty handsome in the dark blue suit that enhanced his light blue eyes. His dirty blond hair was spiked from all of the gel he used. She didn't like that part so much—her hand usually got stuck when she tried to run it through his hair. She stared at his mouth, hoping he would get the hint.

Kiss me! Nono is watching!

"Hey babe," he said. He kissed Natalie on the cheek and walked right by her. "I have to take a piss." He walked down the hallway to the bathroom.

Fudge!

Federico turned to Natalie. "*Very* romantic."

"He kissed me."

"That was, how do you call it? A drive-by kiss?"

"But it was a kiss."

"On the cheek."

She frowned. "I get distracted too when I have to pee."

Jacks finished his business in the bathroom and headed straight for the kitchen. He pointed to the ham in the pan. "Smells good enough to eat." He leaned closer to the kitchen window and pointed outside. "What's that joker doing?"

Federico and Natalie went to the kitchen window and looked out with Jacks.

Giovanni was in his side yard in his underwear, staring down into the garbage can. He placed a box of matches on top of the recycle bin and opened a can of lighter fluid.

Natalie was shocked to see the man she almost gave a ticket to for abandoning his car on the street.

Practically naked.

She didn't want to check him out, but it was impossible to ignore that he was well built with everything in the right place. His muscles had definition but not too much bulk. He wasn't as tall as Jacks, but definitely close to six feet. A fine specimen indeed.

Federico nodded. "That's Giovanni, my wonderful neighbor. He was supposed to get married today. By the looks of things it didn't happen."

They watched as Giovanni paced back and forth in front of the garbage can in his red boxer briefs. He was talking to himself but they couldn't hear what he was saying.

Natalie let out a sympathetic moan. "Poor guy."

"Poor guy nothing," said Jacks. "Looks like you're going to have to arrest him."

"What?"

"That's reckless burning and he doesn't own those receptacles, so we're also talking destruction of city property." Jacks watched Giovanni closely through the window. "Set that fire and you go to jail."

Natalie just stared at Jacks. Sometimes it seemed as if he didn't have a heart. The poor guy got dumped on his wedding day! Giovanni raised the can of lighter fluid over the garbage can, obviously ready to soak whatever was inside.

Natalie knocked loudly on the window to get his attention.

Giovanni jumped and looked over the fence towards Federico's house, making eye contact with Natalie. His black eyes were a perfect match for his hair. He looked down at his underwear and slowly moved behind the garbage can.

"Why did you do that?" asked Jacks.

"So he doesn't do it! You *want* him to start a fire? Where's your compassion?"

Giovanni closed the top of the lighter fluid can, grabbed the box of matches, and slammed the lid shut on the garbage can. He went inside the house and closed the door.

Natalie pretended not to notice his tight, round butt.

A few seconds later Giovanni peeked out the window. Not a very sneaky guy at all.

"I met him today," said Natalie. "I almost gave him a ticket this afternoon for abandoning his car in the middle of the street. He said he was trying to rescue a dog so I let him off."

"What a lame excuse. That guy has issues and was going to set the place on fire. You're going to let him get away with it?"

"He did nothing! He went back in the house. What's your problem?"

"My problem is I'm hungry. And I don't like to see people do things like that. That's how a life of crime begins. They start by breaking the law in small ways and then graduate to carjacking and murder. I've prosecuted people like that before. At least go give him a warning or something."

Natalie sighed. "I'll take care of it."

Jacks stared at Natalie for a moment. "Good." He looked toward the stove again. "Lunch almost ready? I need to take off soon and wash the car before it gets dark."

"Didn't you just wash it two days ago?"

"Yeah. And?"

"Nothing."

Jacks was the overly-proud owner of a 1969 Chevy Camaro. He was obsessed with it—always cleaning it, admiring it, or showing it to somebody so they could admire it too. Sometimes she felt as if he paid more attention to the car than he did to her.

Natalie finished preparing the lunch. She placed the sandwiches on the table for Federico and Jacks and removed her apron. "I'll be right back."

*****

Natalie pulled a fire extinguisher from the trunk of her squad car and walked next door. She admired Giovanni's drought-tolerant front yard of rocks, boulders, and a wide variety of cactus. It looked more like a yard you'd find in Arizona, not Silicon Valley.

She knocked on the door and waited. A few seconds later she heard footsteps inside, followed by the slight opening of the door. Giovanni peeked through the small two-inch opening but didn't speak.

What is this guy doing? Are we playing peekaboo?

"Can I help you?" said Giovanni.

"We need to talk. And I think it would be easier if you open the door a little more."

He opened the door two more inches. "You followed me here?"

"Of course. It's part of our new community service effort.

Just wanted to make sure you got home safe. There have also been reports of indecent exposure in the neighborhood. Have you seen anyone walking around in their yard half-naked?"

"I—"

"That's okay. The real reason I came over is to tell you that using lighter fluid to burn things in your garbage can is against the law."

"I have no idea what you're talking about."

Natalie just stared at him.

"Oh, *lighter* fluid. I thought you said *cider* fluid, as in apple cider. Man, I was thinking…cider fluid is not flammable! And then my next thought was I'm thirsty!"

She continued to stare at him. This typically got people nervous. It's amazing how powerful a lack of words was. Just a few seconds, that's all it took.

He let out a nervous laugh. "You're not going to arrest me, are you?"

"Probably not. Unless you tell another lie…"

"I never actually squirted any lighter fluid in the garbage can. I was about to and—you know—someone saw me. So I stopped."

Giovanni looked over her shoulder to the street. "That guy's staring over here."

She turned around and saw Jacks walking to his car, eating his sandwich.

"Arrest him!" said Jacks with his mouth full. He pulled a

few leaves off the hood of his car, got in, and drove off.

No kiss goodbye. No *thanks for the lunch.* No *I love you.* Nothing. Natalie thought of what her conversation would be with Nono when she got back. She shook her head in disappointment.

Giovanni pointed to Jacks. "Is he your boyfriend?"

"Fiancé."

"Huh…"

Natalie decided it was best to change topics. "I need to inspect your garbage can."

"You don't have to. I told you I didn't use the lighter fluid."

"Then you have nothing to hide if I take a look, right?"

He studied her for a moment. "Okay. I'm a little indisposed though, as you already know. Can you give me a minute while I get myself pretty?"

Natalie almost laughed but held it in. "Of course."

The guy still had a sense of humor, which was impressive considering what had happened to him. A minute later Giovanni swung open the door for Natalie to enter. He was now wearing a t-shirt, shorts, and flip-flops. Not bad, but she preferred him in his underwear.

Giovanni opened the door a little wider. "Please come in."

"Thank you."

She stepped inside and followed him.

"Jasmine," said Giovanni, not turning around.

"No. Natalie."

Giovanni chuckled and stopped. "No. You smell like jasmine. Natalie."

Natalie felt heat creeping up her neck to her face. "Oh. Of course. You have a good nose."

"Thanks. You too."

Me too? Is he even paying attention to me?

They entered the kitchen and Natalie spotted four shot glasses and a bottle of tequila on the counter.

That explains everything. He's drunk.

Giovanni gathered the glasses and quickly stuck them in the sink. He twisted the top back on the tequila bottle and placed it above the fridge.

He wiped down the counter with a towel then turned around with a nervous smile. "My mother. She has this habit of not cleaning up after herself. I'm working on her though. They can be trained!"

"You live with your mother?"

"Uh…no. She just stopped by…for a quick visit."

How many lies is this guy going to tell?

Natalie pointed to the bottle. "To do tequila shots?"

Giovanni paused for a moment before answering. "Yeah."

Natalie stared at him.

"What?"

"You're lying again."

"What makes you think that?"

She removed the handcuffs from her belt and stepped toward Giovanni.

"Okay, okay, okay. I did the shots. Man, I don't mean to lie. It's totally involuntary, really. Don't I get any sympathy from you? You know I got dumped today. *On* my wedding day. But it's true my mother stopped by—not to celebrate though."

Natalie put the handcuffs back on her belt. "Sorry. Again."

Giovanni shrugged. "Thanks."

The curiosity was killing her. Natalie wanted to know what happened, but she knew it would be in poor taste if she asked. Maybe if she chatted with him, threw him a couple of bones, he would tell her.

"That must be devastating for you. I mean, unless you saw it coming."

Take the bait. Take the bait. I feel terrible for doing this, but take the bait!

"It was my own fault. There were signs. I apparently chose to ignore them."

Bingo.

"What types of signs?"

Giovanni let out a deep breath. "For starters, she made me return her engagement ring to the store. She said the diamond was…too small."

"Oh."

"Yeah."

"How small is too small?"

"A carat."

"Really…"

She casually slid her hand behind her back. No reason for him to see her ring. It was a little bit bigger than a carat. Okay, maybe double. But it wasn't as if she picked it out!

Giovanni tried to glance behind her. "What are you hiding back there?"

Fudge!

Natalie swallowed hard. "Nothing."

"Right. That rock on your finger is bigger than a carat, isn't it?"

Natalie shrugged.

"Two carats?"

She shrugged. "Yes, but it's not what you think."

"Hey, I'm not here to judge."

"Seriously. I wanted a smaller diamond. My fiancé insisted. He wanted people to notice."

"It worked. I noticed." Giovanni leaned against the counter. "You see? I don't get that. Shouldn't the goal of a person in love be to always put the other person first? To try to give that person the things they love? The things that make them happy?"

"I—"

"Of course it is! What makes them happy? Find out and give them *that*. And lots of it. The only thing that seemed to make my ex happy was to have what everyone else had. If it was popular, especially expensive, she wanted it. But those are just material things, you know?"

Oh boy. He must be drunk for sure. He's starting to ramble.

"It's a temporary high that doesn't last," continued Giovanni. "You look for the next best thing. And the next. And the next. It's like an addiction. I tried to make her happy, believe me. But she never was. She always wanted more and more. It was never enough."

He was really on a roll now. Should she cut him off or wait until he ran out of steam?

"Maybe you can relate—your fiancé bought you a ring with a diamond the size of a golf ball."

Natalie had the sudden urge to punch the guy.

Instead she fidgeted with her hands and then put them on her hips. "That's not fair. He's…the perfect match for me. Really. That's why I'm marrying him."

Giovanni chuckled. "Yeah. I hear the words coming out of your mouth, but your face is telling me a completely different story. Ready to check my garbage can?"

Who does this guy think he is—analyzing me like that?

She had a sudden case of guilt hitting her right in the gut.

Natalie followed Giovanni toward the side door, but stopped just short of it. "Hang on." She pointed to the towels hanging by the stove. "Did you know those towels are fire hazards?"

"How so?"

She walked over to the stove and pinched the bottom of one of the towels hanging over it with two of her fingers. She extended the towel directly over one of the burners. "You have gas burners. Any sudden flame when you're cooking with oil will light this baby up. Kitchen fires started with oil spread quickly and are difficult to put out. Move this towel rack to the other wall."

He saluted her. "Aye aye, Captain!"

She just stared at him.

"If you're trying to intimidate me with that stare, it's working."

"Good."

"By the way, have you ever thought about becoming a firefighter?"

She nodded. "When I was attending career day in high school those were the two careers I narrowed it down to."

"And why did you choose being a cop?"

"I like the uniform."

"Oh…"

"I'm kidding. The day that I was trying to decide which career to pursue someone stole my bike. It upset me so much I figured that was a sign. To try to prevent others from feeling that way."

"So now you protect and serve."

"Exactly."

Natalie had a funny feeling in her stomach. She'd never told anyone that story before and hadn't even thought of that bicycle in years.

She gestured with her hand toward the door. "Lead the way."

"Of course."

They walked outside. Giovanni pointed to the garbage can.

"Go ahead, take a look. Completely dry."

She set the fire extinguisher on the ground, lifted the lid off of the garbage can, and looked inside. She eyed the brown and gold purse on top. "Is that a real Louis Vuitton?"

Giovanni nodded.

"Huh." She moved some things around and pulled out a pair of high heels with red soles. "Louboutins…" She looked back up at Giovanni. "The woman has expensive taste."

"Yeah."

Natalie felt the things inside of the garbage can and rubbed her fingers together. "Okay. All dry." She looked back down into the garbage can, then back to Giovanni. "You know, you should probably just give these things back to her."

He shrugged. "I don't know."

"Well, it's up to you. But if you don't want to you could at least donate them to a charity. There are women who will never be able to afford something like this in their entire lifetime. You can give them an opportunity to have something luxurious at a discount."

Giovanni scratched his head, then looked into the garbage and nodded. "I like it. You're a genius."

Federico suddenly appeared on the other side of the fence. "Yes! Giovanni, that genius is my little bambina!"

Natalie frowned. "Nono, please."

Giovanni did a double take at Federico. "This is the *little* bambina you've talked about?"

"Yes! My granddaughter Natalie."

Giovanni analyzed her for a moment. "I thought she was…smaller."

Natalie cleared her throat. "You calling me fat?"

"What? No! I didn't mean to. I meant…younger. You're his little bambina. I thought you were like ten years old."

Federico laughed. "She will always be my little bambina."

Giovanni squished his eyebrows together. "How is it I've never met you?"

Natalie shrugged. "The truth is I've only been here twice in the last couple of years. How long have you lived here?"

"Almost two years."

"That explains that. I haven't had a life since you've lived here. I had been working the graveyard shift and taking online classes in my free time. I just got promoted to the day shift a few weeks ago."

"She's staying with me until she gets married," said Federico. "And it's a pleasure to have her. Is she not the most beautiful girl in the world?"

"Nono…"

Federico smiled at Giovanni proudly and gestured toward Natalie. "Well?"

Giovanni nodded. "I'm on the verge of passing out from the intenseness of her beauty. Or maybe I'm getting vertigo by staring at that diamond on her finger."

Natalie placed her hand on her belt. "I can still arrest you."

"She's kidding, Giovanni! She has a heart the size of this town."

"Is that right?" asked Giovanni.

Natalie shook her head. "Don't believe him—I can be a total bitch. Don't test me."

Giovanni pointed to her face. "You're trying to hold in a smile, aren't you?"

"No way."

Natalie kept her face serious as long as she could, then burst out laughing.

Giovanni smiled. "Thank you."

"For what?"

"For distracting me. It's been a crazy day."

"You're welcome. Can I give you some advice?"

"Of course."

"I learned this from my wonderful grandfather who is standing behind me. He taught me that whenever I'm having a bad day or when something isn't going my way, to take the focus off of myself and do something nice for somebody else."

"Like what?"

"It could be anything. As you go through your day look for opportunities. It could be just a smile. A few kind words. Or it could be more than that. It's like a miracle drug, trust me."

"I'll give it a shot, thanks."

"You see?" said Federico. "*This* is why I love my bambina so much. She is the kindest person I know, is she not?"

Giovanni winked at Natalie. "She's a peach."

Natalie didn't say anything. She just wanted to wipe that grin off of Giovanni's face. Not because she didn't like it. No, not at all.

It was quite the opposite.

Chapter Four

Giovanni jumped out of bed with more energy than he'd expected. Odd, considering he just got dumped the day before. If things had gone according to plan he would be leaving for his honeymoon today.

Not even close.

Today he was going to try his hardest to be positive. To be a do-gooder. He would look for situations to help out others and take the focus off of his pathetic love life.

Just like Natalie suggested.

He found it fascinating that she motivated him so easily.

He hit the brew button on the coffee machine, popped a couple of slices of bread in the toaster and sat on the bar stool at the kitchen island, opening his laptop. He always enjoyed going through his emails as he ate. He felt productive that way.

He spread some blueberry jam on the toast, took a bite and washed it down with some coffee. He read an email from Music Prodigies of America—the latest edition was about a young genius who played the guitar.

Amazing.

Most music prodigies played the piano, violin, or cello. But one who played the guitar? That was almost unheard of and so cool. And he was a California kid too, which made him even more special.

The kid—James was his name—was an eight-year old living with foster parents. According to the email he was smart and well-behaved. All he wanted to do was play the guitar, which Giovanni found extraordinary.

Giovanni almost choked on his coffee when he saw the picture of James' guitar. It was way too big for him and in horrible condition. Part of the bridge was even coming off. Not to mention that it was a cheap guitar—at most worth forty bucks.

And just like that Giovanni made the decision. He was going to give James a new guitar—one that fit him better. One that would probably sound a thousand times better than the one in the photo.

Giovanni already had a kid's guitar that was eighty percent finished. A client had paid the deposit and then canceled the order after his son lost interest in playing. This was the perfect opportunity. He figured he could finish it in a few days. He smiled at the thought of donating the guitar to the kid.

His cell phone rang and he stared at it on the kitchen counter.

Not going to answer it.

Probably it was his mother anyway, ready to give him another beat-down and he just wasn't in the mood to be called "pussy" again.

The phone said he had two voicemail messages, but he only heard the one call come in. When did he get the other call? He pressed the play button on the phone and turned on the speaker.

"Hi, it's me…"

Giovanni was putting his plate in the sink and froze.

It was Patricia.

"Sorry I didn't show up to the church. I…uh…we're just…different, you know? Anyway…I'll stop by sometime to pick up the things I have at your place."

Click.

Not good. He had just donated all of her things to charity yesterday. Every single thing. Maybe he should have listened to Natalie and just given the stuff back to her. But could somebody really blame Giovanni for what he had done? He was pissed after she embarrassed him at the church. She left him without saying a word! That was a thousand times worse than donating her clothes. Plenty of people would have done the same thing! Still, he was feeling a little guilty for rushing to donate her clothes barely three hours after he walked out of the cathedral.

He wasn't looking forward to having to explain it to her. Not at all.

He deleted the message and played the next one.

"Hi Giovanni dear, it's me, Beatrice. You saved my little Precious yesterday, remember?"

How could he forget? The mouth kisser.

"I have an emergency and really need your help. Please come to my home immediately."

Beatrice left her address and hung up.

He called her back and it went straight to voicemail. She probably was just craving another mouth kiss. Or maybe it was more than that. She sounded quite disturbed and Giovanni didn't want to take a chance. He quickly got dressed and ran out the door. Fortunately she only lived a few blocks away so he could be there in a couple of minutes.

But why didn't she just call 911? It didn't make any sense.

He pulled into Beatrice's driveway, jumped out of the car and ran to the front door. Before he could even knock the door flew open and Beatrice was standing there next to a huge brown suitcase. She took two steps forward and kissed Giovanni on the lips. "*You* are a lifesaver. A super hero! I think you need to have a big S right here." She gently tapped his chest and made a sizzling sound.

Giovanni wiped his mouth. "As I mentioned previously the kisses are not necessary."

"They are for me! Anyway, here's the scoop: I have a flight that leaves in exactly one hour and forty minutes and the person who was supposed to watch Precious just called and canceled at the last minute. I was ready to text you to let you know I left a key under the doormat in the back yard."

Precious came to the door and wagged her tail when she saw Giovanni. She moved closer and leaned on one of

Giovanni's legs, rubbing her head against him like a cat.

He reached down and scratched her on the head. "Hi Precious. How are you?" He almost thought he heard the dog purring.

Giovanni didn't like where this was going. There was no way he was going to play babysitter to a dog. Sure, Precious was cute and Giovanni loved dogs, but that was beside the point.

"I'm sorry, ma'am, I can't do this."

"Please don't ma'am me! Show him how much you love him, Precious."

Precious jumped up on her hind legs, obviously asking Giovanni to pick her up.

Nice trick.

Giovanni picked her up and was promptly greeted with a lick on the chin.

Beatrice pointed to Precious. "She *loves* you! You can't deny that!"

Precious continued to try to move closer to Giovanni's face to lick him more. Giovanni moved his head back and forth from left to right to avoid her tongue.

The dog seemed to have picked up that kissing habit from her owner.

Precious was funny to him and very cute, but still…

Not going to happen.

"I'm not saying that she doesn't like me," said Giovanni. "And yes, I like her too. But I'm in no position to look after a dog."

"You don't have a house?"

"Yes, of course, but—"

"You have cats?"

"No, but—"

"Obviously you don't have allergies…"

He set Precious down. "No, but…"

"So what's the dealio?"

The woman would not let him finish his sentences. And did she just use the word *dealio*?

"You must know that dogs are chick magnets. You looking to meet a woman?"

"I'm going through a breakup."

"Can I be your rebound?"

Did she really just ask that?

"I—"

Beatrice pinched Giovanni on the arm. "I'm joking! Look, I've had way too much coffee this morning so I'm a little hyper."

No kidding.

"I'm going on an Alaskan cruise with my Bunco group. They're probably already at the airport waiting for me. Ten women, feistier than me."

Feistier than Beatrice? Giovanni didn't think that was possible. He turned and looked behind him as he heard the taxi pull up. He didn't like the feeling building in his gut.

"Do you get joy out of helping others?"

Giovanni knew this was a trick question. "Of course."

"Then it's settled! Thank you!" She leaned forward to kiss Giovanni on the lips again.

He turned at the last second, feeling the impact of her mouth hitting his cheek this time.

She pulled away and looked disappointed. She obviously wanted more lip action. She handed Giovanni a paper with some directions about the dog's daily routines and care and hauled her suitcase toward the taxi.

Beatrice stopped and looked back. "I'll be back in two weeks. The house key is on the kitchen counter and check to make sure all of the windows are closed. Don't forget her food and bowls. Thank you! You get fifty dollars a day."

"I don't need your money, Beatrice."

"Non-negotiable. And please eat everything that's left in the fridge."

And just like that the taxi disappeared down the street, along with Beatrice.

What the hell just happened?

Giovanni stared at Precious who was wagging her cute little tail.

He picked her up again and smiled. "Looks like I have a temporary dog." She licked the side of his face. "How did that happen?"

The truth was Giovanni didn't feel so bad.

This was what Natalie talked about—doing something kind for someone else. Sure, he should've been married now and on his way to Barbados for his honeymoon, but for some reason he felt a sudden rush of peace. Was it coming from Precious?

Precious looked into Giovanni's eyes as if she adored him.

Giovanni smiled.

Maybe taking care of Precious wouldn't be such a bad thing. And it would be a welcome distraction.

*****

Giovanni arrived back home and introduced Precious to her new playground. She ran around exploring every room in the house and sniffing every piece of furniture she encountered. Satisfied, she jumped on the recliner in the living room to rest.

"That's off limits, Precious." She obviously had a hearing problem—she didn't budge. "You hear me? You can have your run of the house and enjoy it, but I have two places that are off limits to you in this house. My bed and that recliner. Got it?"

Precious batted her eyelashes and let out a soft bark.

"And your cuteness will get you nowhere."

Giovanni couldn't believe he was trying to have a conversation with a dog for the second time in two days.

Precious barked again and dropped her chin down on her paws, not moving from the recliner.

He picked her up and placed her on the floor. A few

seconds later she jumped back up on the recliner and laid her head down again, closing her eyes.

Giovanni smiled. How could he have a problem with something so cute? He was pretty sure he just lost his chair for good.

He walked to the side door of the house and inhaled through his nose. He smelled smoke and wondered if his garbage can had caught on fire. He would be in real trouble. None of the lighter fluid dripped out of the can, so that wouldn't make sense if it had. He opened the door and walked outside.

Precious had relinquished the throne and decided to join him.

Giovanni glanced over the fence. Natalie was raking leaves on to a flaming pile.

Giovanni moved closer to the fence and rested his arms along the top of it, watching her work.

Natalie looked much different out of her cop uniform. She wore purple shorts and a purple tank top that hugged her body. Her wavy brown hair was now down, a little below her shoulders, and swayed back and forth as she raked.

Very attractive.

As if she knew she was being watched, she turned around, catching Giovanni staring at her legs.

Son of a biscuit!

Giovanni felt his face burn as he tried to think of something to say to play off his leg-gawking. "Did I miss the invitation for the pyromaniacs meeting?"

She smiled and walked toward him.

Giovanni did his best to maintain eye contact with her. It wasn't easy considering the tanned and toned legs walking in his direction.

She leaned the rake against the fence. "You can kid all you want, but *my* fire is actually legal on county land. Yours yesterday? Not so much."

Giovanni nodded. "Well, technically I didn't have a fire yesterday thanks to someone who was kind enough to point out that I was an idiot."

"Let's just say you had a lapse in good judgment. But it's not a surprise considering what you went through."

Her smile paralyzed him. He had to take a breath before he could speak. "Thanks for understanding."

They had a brief moment there without words. He was sure of it. It almost felt like a connection or something, but that was crazy. The woman was getting married and Giovanni should be in mourning right now. The odd thing was…he wasn't. It was as if he had expected the breakup to happen and had been in denial. There had been signs, red flags, and warnings all over the place with Patricia but he chose to ignore every last one.

I'm an idiot.

Natalie pointed to the dog. "What a cutie pie. What's her name?"

"Precious."

Natalie laughed. "Please tell me you didn't name her that."

"A little too girly?"

"Just a bit. But it actually fits her."

"I would like to take the credit but Precious is not mine. I'm just watching her."

Precious sensed they were talking about her and decided to play cute, licking Giovanni on the chin.

"Stop that, Precious."

"She sure seems to like you."

"Yeah." Giovanni looked toward the house. "Where's Federico?"

"He went to go pick up some Italian sausage. We're having a little barbecue later."

Giovanni nodded again.

Natalie opened her mouth and then closed it.

What was she going to say?

She took the rake and smiled at Giovanni. "You're welcome to come, you know. One o'clock at Strawberry Field. The bocce's always fun."

"I don't know…"

It sounded like an invitation out of pity. She probably felt sorry for him.

She smiled again. "Well, the invite is there for you. In case you change your mind or make up your mind. You can bring Precious too—the park allows dogs."

That was a nice smile. Okay, maybe it wasn't out of pity.

He watched her head back to work. He didn't want to seem like a pervert so he glanced away and went back inside with Precious.

Maybe the barbecue wouldn't be such a bad idea. If anything it would be an excellent way for Giovanni to avoid his mother. Just in case she was in the mood to stop by again and call him names.

Right. Who was he kidding? The real reason to go to the barbecue was to see Natalie again. She had the amazing ability of making him forget about his problems.

Chapter Five

Precious was in sniff-mode as she entered Strawberry Park with her newly-appointed babysitter. Giovanni looked around at all of the people, some playing bocce, some eating, and some drinking. Everyone seemed to be enjoying themselves and it was a beautiful day—clear and in the mid-seventies.

Natalie was talking with a man by the picnic tables. He turned to grab his phone from the table and Giovanni could see it was her fiancé.

Natalie's purple dress hung just above her knees and was covered with tiny white flowers. Her white sandals made her legs look more tanned. Her fiancé was wearing white slacks and a purple polo shirt. Natalie and Jacks were matching and for a moment Giovanni felt a pang of jealousy.

Or was it envy?

Federico approached and handed Giovanni a ball. "Glad you could make it! Who is this little lady?"

"This is Precious. I'm babysitting her for a couple of weeks."

Federico grabbed her tiny paw and rubbed it. "Hello Precious." He looked to Giovanni. "You ever played bocce before?"

"Never."

"Okay. The first thing I will tell you is my balls are green."

Giovanni raised an eyebrow. "You may want to see a doctor about that."

Federico laughed. "That's funny!" He pointed down the court. "You need to get your balls closer to the jack than mine. Then you get points!"

"The jack?"

Federico set his plastic cup of wine down on the table and pointed down the court. "The jack is the smaller ball. You see it? Since my ball is against the jack, knock it out of the way! Got it?"

"Seems easy enough."

Giovanni handed the leash to Federico. He took careful aim and rolled the ball down the court. The ball rolled directly at Federico's ball and knocked it out of the way, exposing the jack.

Federico jumped with excitement and slapped Giovanni on the back. "Yes! That's how you do it!"

Giovanni's lip curled up just a tad.

Federico pointed to his mouth. "I think I saw a smile!

"Give me another ball."

"Of course!"

Federico handed him another ball. Giovanni stepped up, even more serious than the first time and threw the ball down the court. It glided slowly and stopped just an inch from the jack.

Federico slapped him on the back again. "Benissimo! You are a natural, my friend."

Giovanni let out a small smile. "I kind of like this game."

"Of course you do! This game goes all the way back to the Roman Empire. What a way to forget about your problems for a while, no?"

"Yeah."

"Sometimes it also helps you realize that what you believe are problems are actually blessings in disguise."

Giovanni liked Federico. He was always so upbeat and generous.

"Thanks, Federico."

"Not at all, my friend." Federico reached down to pet Precious on the head and caught Giovanni staring at him when he stood back up. "Why do you look at me that way?"

Giovanni shrugged his shoulders. "I don't know. I guess I'm just wondering how you can be so upbeat all the time."

"Why not?"

"Well, if my wife had just died…"

Federico didn't answer and handed Giovanni the leash.

"Sorry, stupid question. I'm sorry, Federico."

Federico waved him off and took another sip. "No, no, no. It's not stupid at all. What might sound stupid is my answer. You see, Olive is still with me, every minute, every day, right here." Federico put his hand over his heart and smiled. "I have the most beautiful memories of our years together and if I concentrate hard enough, really hard, it's as though I am reliving them again one by one."

Giovanni nodded and smiled. "I like that. You're a good guy, Federico."

"Grazie. You too. You ready for more bocce?"

"Yeah. Although I think it would be unfair if I didn't give you an opportunity to smack my balls around."

"I seriously hope you're talking about bocce balls," said Natalie. She smiled and kissed Federico on the cheek. "Hi Nono."

Natalie looked even more beautiful close up. She was wearing a purple bracelet and purple earrings that matched her dress.

She looked good in purple.

"Picolina," said Federico. "Did you get enough to eat?"

Natalie frowned. "Too much. Hi Precious." She scratched the dog under the chin and Precious licked her hand.

Federico pointed to Natalie. "Giovanni, of course you remember my beautiful granddaughter?"

Giovanni smiled. "How can I forget?"

"Do I note a hint of sarcasm again?"

"Nooooooooo. Me?"

Giovanni and Natalie smiled at each other as Jacks joined them.

Natalie gestured to Jacks. "Giovanni, this is my fiancé... Jacks."

Giovanni held out his hand. "Nice to meet you. Jacks?"

"Yes sir."

"With an s?"

"That's right."

Giovanni held in the laughter. The guy was plural.

As if Jacks knew what Giovanni was thinking he squeezed his hand tighter. "It's short for Jackson." He let go of Giovanni's hand and pointed to the parking lot. "Some people have been asking to check out the car. You want to see it?"

Giovanni glanced over to the parking lot and then back to Jacks. "The Camaro?"

Jacks nodded. "Not just any Camaro. It's a 1969 ZL1. Mint condition. Only sixty-nine of them in the world."

Big deal. "I didn't know that. But I'll pass."

Jacks cocked his head to the side. "You sure?"

"Yes. There's only one Federico in the world and I want to enjoy his company."

Giovanni glanced at Natalie and saw her smile.

"You are so kind!" said Federico.

Jacks scratched his jaw. "It's got a four hundred twenty-seven cubic inch V-8."

"That's nice," said Giovanni. "My next car isn't going to have an engine at all."

Natalie perked up. "You're going to buy an electric car?"

Giovanni nodded.

Natalie smiled. "Me too!"

Jacks gave up and walked in the direction of his car.

Giovanni glanced over to Natalie who was grinning.

She quickly looked to Federico. "You may want to throw a few more sausages on the barbecue."

Federico shrugged. "I was going to but we don't have any more."

Natalie's face turned a very lovely shade of pink. "That would probably be my fault. I can't remember if I had two or three."

Federico stared at Natalie, waiting.

Natalie let out a nervous laugh. "Okay, I had three. Who am I kidding? I can't help it. They're the best."

A woman who liked to eat. Giovanni liked that. None of that salad-a-day diet crap.

He looked over at the food table and then back to Federico. "I can go pick up a few more sausages."

Federico lit up and placed his hand on Giovanni's shoulder. "That would be wonderful! We get them from a secret place so Natalie can show you where you need to go."

Natalie glanced over at Jacks who already had the hood open on his car. "Okay."

A minute later Giovanni and Natalie were in the car. Precious was in the back seat.

Giovanni glanced over at Natalie as they sat at a red light. "Is there really a secret sausage place?"

"*Top* secret."

He looked over to her again and got his eyes back on the road as the light changed to green. "Really…"

"That's right."

"So, down a back alley or something? With secret passwords and armed guards?"

"Not quite. Make a left at the next light."

"Okay."

"How are you doing, by the way?"

"I'm fine. How are you?"

"Okay, let me rephrase that. I mean, how are you *feeling?* You know—after yesterday."

"Oh. That."

He really was in no mood to talk about that.

"If you don't want to talk about it, that's okay."

She's a mind reader, but Giovanni knew he should say something. "Well…I haven't sunk into a deep depression yet if that's what you're wondering."

"Maybe you're in denial."

"Not even close. I came to a pretty fast realization that *that* marriage was an accident waiting to happen. Her not showing up was probably the best thing that could have happened. It's just…well. It's embarrassing."

"Yeah… Make a left here and stop in front of the green house on the right."

Giovanni did a double take at the house. "This place? Seriously?"

"Yes. Seriously."

The house was the ugliest shade of green he'd ever seen. There were bars over the windows and a front yard that was just dirt. Someone decided to park their old Volkswagen Bug on the dirt. A man walked out of the house with a bag and quickly got in his car and took off.

Giovanni glanced over to Natalie. "Don't tell me—your family is in the Italian sausage black market and the sausage is stolen. Does the Mafia run this place?"

Natalie laughed. "Keep the engine running."

"Of course. Just like a bank robbery. If someone calls the cops I don't know you. Hey, wouldn't that be weird if someone called the cops on us and the dispatcher contacted you to go investigate?"

"I'm not on the clock. And you watch too much television." She disappeared into the house for not more than a minute before returning with a paper bag. She got back in the car and used her thumb to point behind them. "Go! Go! Go!"

Giovanni freaked out and stepped on the gas. "What the hell is going on?"

Natalie laughed and grabbed his arm. "Calm down or you're going to get a ticket. I was just kidding. Relax."

He loved Natalie's laugh. It was full and hearty.

Giovanni smiled. "You're crazy."

"I'm just having fun. The truth is a woman named Anita lives there. She's been making sausages for over thirty years —she turned her garage into a mini-factory. She supplies them to a few restaurants and markets. It's a small operation but they are the best in the world! My grandfather used to be good friends with her late husband so she insists on giving us sausages. I'm not going to say no, either. I think I'll have another one when we get back. Or ten."

Natalie was cool. You'd never know she was a cop if you didn't see her in uniform. Maybe a high school teacher. Or a Zumba instructor.

Giovanni opened his mouth and closed it.

"What?" said Natalie.

"Nothing."

"Tell me."

"Okay. Your fiancé doesn't seem to have the same sense of humor you have. Or sense of adventure."

Natalie didn't answer.

"He seems kind of serious."

"He has a very stressful job. He's a prosecuting attorney."

"And he *really* likes his car."

She nodded. "That's an understatement."

"How's your wedding stuff going? You planning on showing up?"

Natalie laughed. "Yes, of course I plan to show up. Why wouldn't I?"

"I was joking." *Not really.* "But…you don't seem very close to him."

"You don't even know me."

"That's a good point, but some things can be pretty obvious."

Hopefully she wouldn't take it too personal. Something

wasn't right with the two of them, he was sure of it. Was it a marriage of convenience? Or maybe she was pregnant. He used the opportunity at the stop sign to casually drop his gaze to her belly.

She cocked her head to the side. "I'm not pregnant!"

Shit.

Women were too smart.

"I didn't say you were pregnant."

"You didn't have to. Look, I'm getting married to him because he's a good man."

"Is *good* good enough?"

"I meant to say great. It's just that I'm a little overwhelmed with the planning. I did most of it and he's not around much. I want everything to be perfect and he's not helping. So if something goes wrong it's my fault."

"Maybe you should elope."

"Too late now."

"Yeah. Too late for me too."

Natalie smiled.

"There's so much pressure to get married."

"You had pressure?"

"More than you'll know. From my mother."

She laughed. "You're a man."

"And?"

She shrugged. "Nothing. I just never heard of a guy getting pressure from his mother to get married."

"You've never met my mother. And by the way, that's

probably a good thing." He thought about his mom for a moment. "She calls me names."

Shit. Why did I tell her that?

Natalie turned and Giovanni could feel her eyes on him but she wasn't speaking. Did he have something hanging out of his nose? Damn. He couldn't wipe it now. She'd notice for sure.

Turn away! Quit looking in my direction! Nothing to see here!

Natalie placed her hand on Giovanni's shoulder and squeezed it. "Sorry."

"It's no big deal."

"Yes, it is. It's amazing to me that a parent would call their child names. What does she call you?"

He shrugged. "Pussy."

Natalie's hand flew to her chest. "Please tell me you're joking."

He shook his head.

"God. The woman's got issues. And you must have a lot of issues too with a mother like that."

Giovanni laughed. "Surprisingly, no. I can't complain about my life at all. The only problem I have is choosing women who don't realize that it's okay to break up with someone before the groom arrives at the church."

Natalie smiled and squeezed his shoulder again. "You'll find someone else. You're very nice…and non-psychotic. Unlike your mother."

Giovanni laughed. "Gee, thanks."

"My pleasure."

Precious jumped from one side of the back seat to the other. "Arf! Arf!"

Natalie tried to look back at her but the dog was directly behind her seat. "What's she up to?"

Hopefully the dog wasn't taking a crap in the car.

Giovanni looked back at Precious. "I'm not sure—her tail is wagging. She's excited about something. Maybe she has to pee."

"Arf! Arf!"

Natalie pointed to the dog park. "Or wants to play."

Giovanni pulled to the side of the road and turned off the engine. "Okay, just a quick visit."

"Uh…"

"Sorry. Do you want to go back to the barbecue?"

Natalie looked over at the dog park. "No, no. It's okay—let's go."

Giovanni wondered why she was hesitant with her answer. She definitely didn't have a fear of dogs because she petted Precious when they met. They got out of the car and Precious pulled hard toward the entrance of the dog park.

"Looks like she's been here before," said Natalie.

"Precious!" yelled an older woman with a labradoodle, confirming Natalie's statement. "Where's your mama?" The woman looked to Giovanni for an answer.

"Beatrice went on vacation and asked me to look after her."

"Well, bless your heart. Come here."

Oh God no, not another eager-senior-citizen-mouth-kisser. "Pardon me?"

The woman reached into her fanny pack and pulled out some treats. "Precious loves these. Tell her to sit first, though. She's a smart girl."

"Oh"

Thank God. False alarm. No kissing.

The woman stuck two fingers in her mouth and whistled like a high school football coach. "Precious! Here!"

Precious sprinted toward the woman and came to a stop right in front of her. She'd done this before.

The woman turned to Giovanni. "Okay, hold a treat above her and ask her to sit."

Giovanni took the treat from the woman's hand and held it in the air. "Precious, sit."

Precious sat and Giovanni smiled. "Very cool."

"Now don't just stand there, reward her!"

"Oh!" Giovanni bent down and held the treat in the palm of his hand for Precious. The dog gently grabbed it with her mouth and chewed.

The woman handed Giovanni a handful of treats. "Here's a few more. You can get them down at the pet store on University Avenue. Have fun!"

Giovanni waved goodbye to the woman and sat down on the bench with Natalie.

Precious took off again, running around with some of the

other dogs. A labradoodle, a pug, and a yellow lab seemed to be her favorite play buddies.

Natalie looked over to Giovanni. "I'll be back."

"Okay."

What was she going to do? Natalie walked toward the large oak tree in the center of the dog park and reached down to pet a golden retriever. She smiled as she talked with the owner of the dog. She stroked the dog a few more times and then wandered back to Giovanni with a smile on her face. A very beautiful, natural smile.

"I haven't set foot inside of a dog park in a *very* long time," she said.

"Yeah? How long?"

She sat back down on the bench next to Giovanni. "Fifteen years. Ever since my dog died, well, you know…"

"Yeah. That can be tough. Some people love their dogs more than some of their family members."

"That's just it, he was family. I loved him very much."

"That's sweet. What kind of dog?"

"Golden retriever. Just like that one over there. His name was Hairy." Giovanni laughed and Natalie smacked him on the arm. "Hey! Don't laugh!"

"What do you expect?" He pointed to Precious. "You made fun of her when you found out her name? Ha! Hairy…"

"No. I made fun of *you*."

"Okay, maybe you did."

"Anyway, Hairy was my best friend. He slept in my room every night—his bed was right next to mine. When he died I thought I'd never want a dog again. Why go through that agony again when he dies, right?"

Giovanni nodded.

"I got over it. Enough so that I was ready to get another dog, but…Jacks hates dogs."

"How could a person hate dogs?"

She shrugged.

"I can understand if you have a preference for cats or another animal maybe, but dogs are beautiful creatures."

"I agree."

The cute little pug waltzed over and licked Natalie's leg. She reached down and stroked it.

Giovanni pointed to the dog. "This dog likes you a lot."

"Yeah. Well, I like him too."

"He could actually be reincarnated Hairy."

Natalie laughed. "He came back as a pug?"

"Why not?" The pug sat and leaned against Natalie's leg. "It could happen. Look at him—he has fifty dogs to play with and he would rather be with you."

She rubbed him under his chin. "He sure is cute." Natalie almost looked a little sad, as though she were longing to have a dog again.

"So no dog for you then?"

She shrugged. "I can just dream about them."

"If it'll make you feel better you can babysit Precious for a few days."

"Nice try!"

Giovanni laughed. "It was worth a shot."

"You can pretend you're not that into her, but I can see it. You like her."

"Maybe."

He did like Precious. She was cute and smart and loyal. And he knew there was no way she would leave him at the altar. Wait. Where the hell did that come from?

Precious came running back and jumped on Giovanni's lap.

He scratched her on the head. "Hey girl. You having fun?"

She wagged her tail and licked him on his hand.

"I think she wants another treat," said Natalie.

"Oh." Giovanni set Precious on the ground and reached for a couple more treats. He stood up, towering over Precious. "Sit."

Precious sat and stared at him with her beautiful doggie eyes.

"Let's experiment a little bit here." Giovanni held out his hand. "Shake."

Precious gave him her left paw.

"Wow! And the other paw?"

Precious switched and gave him the right paw. Natalie smiled and applauded.

"Very good!" said Giovanni. He gave her a treat. "You're such a smart girl, aren't you?"

Giovanni reached down and picked up Precious, resting her against his chest. She thanked him for the lift by licking him on his chin. "We should probably get back to the barbecue."

Natalie stood up and nodded. "Yeah, I'm sure Jacks is wondering where the heck I am."

A few minutes later they arrived back at Strawberry Park and Natalie handed the sausage to Federico.

"Grazie!"

"You're welcome, Nono."

Federico opened the bag and placed a few of the sausages on the barbecue. Natalie looked over to Jacks who finally had closed the hood of his car. He walked over, pulled out his cell phone, and sat on top of the picnic table.

"Sorry it took so long," said Natalie. "We had an unexpected delay with the dog."

Jacks scrolled a little more on his phone and looked up. "What are you talking about?"

She shrugged. "Nothing. It's just we didn't plan on being gone so long."

He raised an eyebrow. "You left?"

"Yeah. Never mind."

"Okay."

He dropped his head to concentrate on whatever he was doing on his phone again.

Giovanni saw the frustrated look on Natalie's face. If Jacks was her fiancé he sure wasn't acting like it. There was no connection, no spark, no passion. Nothing.

Natalie forced a smile at Giovanni and reached down to pet Precious. Giovanni didn't know Natalie very well, but he did know this; she was sweet and kind and considerate. She let him off the hook with that ticket so she was compassionate too.

He studied her from head to toe. And she was hot as hell.

Uh oh.

What just happened there? He shouldn't be checking out a woman who was getting married.

Stop looking at her!

Giovanni needed to clear his head. He looked around the park. "Where are the restrooms?"

Natalie popped up. "I'll show you."

Giovanni's imagination must have been playing tricks on him—he was almost certain that she really wanted to escape again. She was way too excited about the restrooms.

Yeah, something is definitely wrong with their relationship. And they're getting married soon. He wouldn't be surprised if one of them didn't show up.

They walked to the restrooms and Giovanni couldn't help but say something. "How did you meet Jacks?"

"I testified in a case he was prosecuting."

Hopefully Giovanni didn't piss her off but he wanted to know more. "How long have you known each other?"

Natalie tucked some hair behind one of her ears. "Six months."

"Oh…"

They both watched as Precious squatted and did her business.

Giovanni reached down to scoop up the nuggets into a poop bag. "Second poop in an hour! Is that normal?"

Natalie smiled. "No. You must inspire her."

Giovanni laughed. "I'm not sure how to take that." He tossed the poop bag in the trash and scratched Precious on her lower back near her tail. "Feel better, Precious? Of course you do. And a pound lighter I would imagine."

Natalie laughed. "It wasn't *that* big. Don't give her a complex."

"Sorry, Precious. How insensitive of me."

They continued toward the restrooms and Giovanni handed Natalie the leash while he went inside. When he was done he took the leash back from her. "Your turn."

"Oh…I don't really have to go."

Giovanni nodded and joked. "Couldn't pass up an opportunity to spend more time with me, huh?"

Natalie opened her mouth and then closed it.

"What?" asked Giovanni.

"Nothing."

"Something. Say it."

They strolled back toward the picnic area, occasionally stopping when Precious wanted to sniff something.

Natalie chuckled. "Okay. I was just going to ask you…you said there were signs that you knew maybe you weren't in a good relationship. What signs?"

He knew it. It sounded like someone was having some doubts.

Giovanni thought about it. "I don't know. Things like not paying attention to the little details. Or just not paying attention to me much. I don't mind people being on their smart phones now and then, but it seemed like she was always glued to that thing. Even when we were out for what I thought was a romantic dinner or at a family gathering."

He saw Natalie glance back to the picnic area. Jacks was still on his phone.

He felt guilty. He didn't want to make her feel bad and he didn't know the entire story with her and Jacks. One thing he knew for sure, he was enjoying her company.

He felt another pang of guilt.

Was he hoping she didn't get married? Yeah, maybe he was. But that wasn't fair that he would wish that upon her just because he went through it. Not fair at all.

"Sorry," he said. "Probably not a good topic. You're getting married soon."

"Yeah…"

"How soon?"

"Two weeks."

"Oh wow."

"I have my bachelorette party tomorrow."

"Strippers and booze and all that?"

"No way. My best friend Rebecca wanted strippers and I

nixed that. We're just going out for dinner and drinks. Nice and simple."

"We ended up playing poker in the clubhouse at the apartment complex of a friend. Just like you, nice and simple. My friend Stevie wanted to go to Vegas for a week."

"Boys will be boys. Jacks…"

Giovanni leaned in to take a closer look at Natalie's face. "Yes? Jacks?"

"Well…Jacks is, uh, going to Vegas."

"Oh…"

They walked back to the picnic area where Jacks was still on his phone.

Giovanni whispered. "Sounds like you and I have a lot in common."

She didn't have a response to that.

It was a much better afternoon than Giovanni had anticipated. He enjoyed Natalie's company. A little too much. He was already wondering when he would get to see her again.

And he was sure thoughts like those would spell trouble on the horizon.

Chapter Six

Natalie stood up from the kitchen table and cleared a few plates. "Thanks, Nono. The pancakes were amazing. Where did you learn to make those? From Grandma?"

"Ancient Chinese secret."

She laughed. "Right." She placed the plates in the dishwasher and glanced out the window toward Giovanni's house. He was a really nice guy.

Kind. Handsome.

Sure, she couldn't help but notice. Just because she was engaged didn't mean she couldn't appreciate the opposite sex. As long as she didn't stare or touch.

Giovanni came out the side door of his house and saw Natalie.

Speak of the devil.

Their eyes locked for a few seconds.

Bam!

She felt something in her heart and pressed her hand to her chest. What was that? Okay, maybe she was attracted to him. A little.

She waved to him.

He smiled and waved back.

Bam!

She felt something again. This time in the pit of her stomach.

Giovanni walked toward the back of his yard and disappeared inside of what appeared to be a cottage.

Natalie turned back to her grandfather. "What's that small building in the back of Giovanni's yard? Like a guest house or something?"

Federico walked to the window and looked out. "No, no, no. Did I not mention it to you? That man is a musical genius. And *that* is the studio where he works."

Natalie tilted her head to the side. "What do you mean? Like, he's a musician?"

"Well, yes and no. Yes, he is a musician. He plays the guitar and very well, I might add. But what I am speaking of is far more creative than that."

"Okay, you've built up the suspense enough, so please tell me."

"He builds the most *beautiful* guitars in the world."

"In the world? Could you be exaggerating just a little?"

He shook his head. "And he makes them with his hands."

"Really?" She stared back at the little studio in his yard. "Wow. That's a very unique profession."

She stared at Federico for a moment and then turned her attention back to the studio. She realized that during the few moments she and Giovanni had spent together he never once mentioned what he did or bragged about his accomplishments. If he truly were a genius, he was a *down-to-earth* one and Natalie liked that. Jacks was always talking about his job and it really got old after a while.

Natalie cleared her throat. "Um…if you know him so well and like him so much, how come you weren't invited to his wedding?"

"Ahh," said Federico, scratching his chin. "This is a very good question. I don't have an answer."

She stared over the fence into Giovanni's yard.

Federico pointed to Giovanni's studio. "Go visit him."

"What? No! Why would I do that?"

"Because you are curious, I can see it. I sometimes go and watch him work, for hours even. He doesn't mind at all. Come with me."

"Over there? No!"

"Yes."

He reached for her hand and they walked to the backyard.

Natalie tried to pull her hand free. "He's probably very busy. We shouldn't disturb him."

"Nonsense. He has an open door policy to the world. That's who he is."

They walked to the back of Federico's yard behind the lemon tree where Federico opened a gate.

"I never noticed this gate before. Did you install this recently?"

Federico laughed. "Of course not." He stepped through the gate and waved Natalie through. "The original owner of my property also owned Giovanni's property. His sister lived in the other house. He wanted them to connect so the kids would pass back and forth between the properties with ease!"

Federico knocked on the studio door and pushed it open. "Giovanni!"

Some type of Spanish flamenco guitar music was playing on a sound system.

"Good morning, Federico. Come on in."

Giovanni's back was to them so he obviously didn't know that Natalie was with him.

Should she say something?

"Hi Natalie," Giovanni said. He set down a piece of sandpaper and turned around. "How are you?"

How did he do that? Did he have eyes in the back of his head?

"Hello…uh…" She twirled some hair around her index finger for a moment. "How did you know I was here? Your back was turned."

He shrugged. "Jasmine."

Right. He knew the scent of her perfume.

"I love it," continued Giovanni.

"Thank you."

He smiled and winked. "Not at all."

Bam!

Damn that heart. She was going to make an appointment with a cardiologist first thing Monday morning.

Federico placed his hand on Giovanni's shoulder. "I was

telling Natalie that you make the most beautiful guitars in the world."

"You're too kind, Federico. I don't know about that, but thank you. I appreciate it."

"He's just being humble. He has a two-year waiting list for his guitars!"

"Really?" Natalie moved in closer to inspect one of the guitars hanging from a stand. "That's amazing. I heard you play too."

"Yes, it's another one of my passions."

She loved men who were passionate about their careers. Jacks was obsessed.

Big difference.

Stop!

Why was she comparing Giovanni to Jacks again?

Don't go there.

Natalie turned around and Federico was gone. "Where did…?"

"What?" said Giovanni.

"Oh. Nothing."

What was Nono up to?

It was as if he set her up. She knew he didn't really approve of Jacks, but…

Natalie tried to regain her composure and explored the studio, stopping at a beautiful guitar that was sitting on a floor stand. "This looks smaller than the normal guitars."

He picked it up and strummed a few chords. "Very

perceptive of you. I'm making it for an eight year old boy."

"Really?"

Giovanni nodded and handed it to her.

She inspected it and smelled it. "It's beautiful. Smells nice too."

Giovanni laughed. "Yeah, I love smelling the guitars too."

She pointed to the stool. "May I?"

"Of course." He leaned over and brushed some dust off the top of the stool with his hand. "Please."

"It's so peaceful in here."

"That's by design. This is my trade, but it's almost a form of meditation when I am working. The worst possible thing could be happening in my life, but when I'm in here I disconnect. It's just me and the guitars."

"I like that. Maybe I should come here when I have a stressful day."

Giovanni pointed to the door. "The door's always open when I'm here."

"Yeah, that's what my grandfather told me. How long does it take you to make each guitar?"

"It's about a month of labor, but that's not continuous time. Each guitar is in various stages and I typically work on three at the same time. If you actually count the time from start to finish, my clients get their new guitars about six months after I start working on them."

"A whole month of labor." She looked around the studio. "For just one."

"There are so many little things that go into making a guitar. It's not like a big factory with giant machines that do most of the work. Every step takes time and patience. There's only one of me and each and every guitar is a piece of me."

"And you make a living off of this?"

He nodded. "I do okay."

They locked eyes and she started twirling hair again.

"Are you working on your curls?"

Fudge!

Natalie was a little nervous but she wasn't going to admit it to Giovanni. What a disaster.

And what a wimp.

She was a cop who has chased bad guys through rat-infested hell-holes. She' tackled and handcuffed criminals bigger than linemen for the Forty-Niners. But in this tiny studio with this good-looking, guitar making Greek god—or maybe he was Italian—she was mush.

Complete, one hundred percent mush.

It was time for her to make a swift exit before she said or did something she regretted. "Gotta run. Thanks for showing me your studio."

"Anytime. My pleasure."

Pleasure. That sounds enticing. I need more of that. A couple of orders of that would be wonderful.

When was the last time she had sex, anyway? Her mind wandered to Giovanni in his underwear, trying to set his garbage can on fire. Did she notice his broad shoulders, muscular legs and flat abs?

Hell yeah, she did.

Giovanni waved his hand in front of Natalie's face. "You okay?"

She was pretty sure her face was now as hot as the surface of the sun.

"Fine!" she said with way too much volume. "See you later."

Natalie made a quick exit.

What just happened in there?

What kind of an engaged woman acted like that? It sure seemed like she was having doubts about things and she felt guilty about it.

She didn't want to hurt Jacks. Nobody deserved to go through what Giovanni did.

Why couldn't relationships be easier?

Yup. She was having doubts alright. Or was it cold feet?

It was cold feet, for sure. Everybody went through this before a wedding. She tried to justify her emotions and find a logical reason for her behavior.

One thing was for sure, she needed to get her act together. She had a bachelorette party tonight and she would be getting married soon. And her girlfriends would know in an instant if she was preoccupied or distracted by something. Which she definitely was.

*****

Giovanni walked to the studio door, peeking outside. Natalie passed through the gate in the back and stopped to smell the roses in Federico's backyard. She took a few more steps and paused again to inspect one of the lemon trees.

Natalie was a beautiful woman. There was a down-to-earth quality she possessed that was very innocent and endearing. Odd, considering she was a cop. He had no doubts though that she could turn on the tough anytime she wanted. Like a light switch.

Giovanni's phone rang and startled him. He tried to jump back inside his studio before Natalie spotted him. Not even close.

Son of a bearded dragon!

He wouldn't blame her if she thought he was some of kind of weirdo.

He checked the caller ID.

It was Stevie and he answered. "Hey."

"Hey," said Stevie. "I was walking by that new French restaurant in downtown last night and—"

"I didn't know there was a new French restaurant. What's it called?"

"Hell, I don't know. Depardieu. Le Pew. Voulez Vous. Something like that, but that's not my point. Can I finish?"

Giovanni sat on the stool and sighed. "By all means."

"Patricia was there."

Giovanni stood back up. "Oh." He paced back and forth in his studio. "Alone?"

Stevie laughed. "Seriously? What a question. She's not going to be alone at some foofoo place like that. She was with a guy. A guy wearing a thousand dollar suit and a Rolex. *And* they were sipping on Cristal. Whoever he was, he's got bank."

Giovanni wasn't surprised and was quite relieved.

Patricia never was the right woman for him.

He always tried to focus on the positives in every person, but that doesn't mean you should completely overlook the negatives. Sometimes things in a relationship were unbalanced and you had to take notice. Still, he did wonder *why* she didn't show up at the wedding. Why she never said a thing.

"Are you there, Giovanni?"

"Yeah."

"Your ex is already out there dating and you've got nothing to say?"

He chuckled. "What do you want me to say? It's really not that big of a surprise to me, now that I think about it. We were two completely different people. I wasn't enough for her. I would have *never* been able to satisfy a woman like that."

"Sexually speaking?"

"*No.* Not sexually speaking."

"So you're okay with this?"

"I'm okay, Stevie. My ego took a big hit when she didn't show up. I was embarrassed, but I'm starting to see things clearly now."

"Wow. Maybe you're getting your balls back, but you still need our support. We're coming over."

"That's not necessary."

Too late. Stevie already hung up.

What Giovanni had told Stevie was the truth. He didn't feel great.

But he also didn't feel shattered or heartbroken.

Giovanni knew he was a good person and it wouldn't be long before he met someone who was meant for him.

He peeked outside of the studio again for Natalie but she was gone. Funny how when he was thinking of meeting someone else he thought of her. He needed to stop doing that. The woman was getting married and it was wrong.

The last thing he wanted was to develop feelings for a woman who would never be his.

Chapter Seven

Giovanni locked the front door of his home and stood on the front porch. He took a deep breath and exhaled slowly. Considering he got dumped recently he wasn't feeling bad at all. He was even alert enough to notice the beautiful hummingbird hovering over his aloe vera plant in the front yard.

He felt good.

Should he be worried about that?

Giovanni had planned on taking three weeks off for the wedding and honeymoon, but now that the wedding was a bust he wasn't going to sit around and watch the time go by. He would spend some of that time working on his guitars, of course. He even got back to work on his latest creation for James.

But that would have to be put on hold until tomorrow. He was being kidnapped by the two stooges waiting for him on the sidewalk.

Danny and Stevie were still convinced that Giovanni needed comfort and support. The three were now on their way to grab an after-dinner coffee and dessert. Why not? It would be good to not stray too far away from the normal routine and the boys always enjoyed hanging out in the evenings whenever they had a chance.

After Giovanni greeted them both with brotherly hugs Stevie unlocked the doors to his classic '58 Cadillac convertible and pointed next door. "Hey, there's Federico."

Danny whispered, "Someone should tell him that plaid hasn't been popular since the fifties."

Giovanni wagged his finger at Danny. "Leave him alone. He's a good guy."

Federico waved. "Giovanni! Buona sera!"

"Hi Federico."

"What are you gentlemen up to on this beautiful evening?"

Giovanni pointed to Stevie and Danny. "They're in the mood for Dolce Spazio. Would you like to join us?"

Federico smiled. "That sounds wonderful, but I'm leaving for a book club meeting." He held up his book. "We will be discussing *The Notebook*. And after that we are going to watch the movie!"

Danny laughed. "I didn't know you read that girly stuff, Federico. My wife reads that."

"It's not just for women, I'm telling you. It's one of the most beautiful stories of my generation. Of *your* generation. It's about—"

"Yadda yadda yadda," said Stevie. "These books give women unrealistic expectations of what love really is about. Next thing you know she's asking you to cuddle and remember her birthday and kiss her on a daily basis and sleep in the wet spot. I don't have time for that nonsense. I'm a busy guy!" He held up a high-five for Giovanni who didn't respond.

"You're an idiot too," said Giovanni. "Don't listen to him, Federico."

"Well, he is entitled to his opinion," said Federico. "It's like I tell my bambina, it takes all kinds to make the world go around."

Giovanni looked over toward Federico's house. "How *is* Natalie?"

"Good—I just talked with her. They are celebrating with the bachelorette party at the Los Gatos Brewing Company this evening."

LGBC is located just down the street from Dolce Spazio—within walking distance—but Giovanni wasn't going to even entertain the thought of going over there.

Giovanni nodded. "You think he's the right one for Natalie?"

He shrugged. "That is for her to decide."

Federico didn't sound very positive on the topic. Giovanni was almost certain they both felt the same way. Jacks wasn't worthy of her.

Federico perked up. "You can stop by and say hi to her, you know?"

Crap.

That just opened the door for Stevie.

Giovanni needed to squash that idea immediately. "No, no. Bachelorette parties are for women and we don't want to interrupt."

Stevie stepped closer and looked serious for a moment. "I think we should. How many girls are we talking about?"

"Here we go…" said Giovanni.

"I'm not sure," said Federico. "I think Natalie mentioned ten to twelve."

Stevie turned back toward the car. "We've hit the jackpot. Let's go."

Giovanni hooked Stevie's arm and yanked him back. "*You* are not going anywhere."

"What? What are you talking about? Federico said it was okay, didn't you?"

Federico nodded and chuckled. "Of course. As long as you don't act like animals I don't see what could be wrong with just saying hello."

"Exactly," said Stevie. "Just saying hello, that's all. And if I happen to get a few phone numbers in the process, even better!" He leaned over to Danny to high-five him and Danny left him hanging as well.

"No," said Giovanni.

These events were sacred for women and the last thing they wanted was a bunch of guys trying to join in or hit on them. Besides, Giovanni felt a strong connection when he spoke with Natalie. She was spunky and fun and a beautiful woman. He was attracted to her, but he would be a masochist to go in there and pretend he had a chance with her.

Hell, he would love a chance with her. To spend more time together. Get to know her even more. But it wasn't going to happen. She was getting married and he needed to leave it alone.

Giovanni smiled at Federico. "Enjoy this evening at your book club."

"Thank you! And you have a wonderful evening too!"

Ten minutes later the boys were seated at a table in Dolce Spazio with their coffees, cookies, cakes, and gelato. Giovanni took a sip of his latte and moaned. "This was a good idea."

"Of course it was," said Danny. "It's good to get out. You can't hide in that guitar-making-man-cave of yours forever."

"Hey, I don't hide in there. I love making those guitars. That's my passion and there's nothing wrong with that. You work too. I just happen to work from home."

"I'm just saying…it's good to get out, that's all."

"Fine. But if anyone even mentions the word 'intervention' I'm leaving."

Stevie winked at an attractive woman in line. She smiled and whispered something to her girlfriend.

"What are you doing?" asked Giovanni.

Stevie kept eye contact with the woman. "I'm just sending out a little signal."

"What type of signal is that? 'Look at me, I'm an idiot!'

That kind?"

"It's called non-verbal flirting. I read about it in a book I just picked up at a garage sale: *Getting the Love You Want Without Having to Pay Through The Nose*. It's also a self-help guide for cocaine addicts. I only paid twenty-five cents for the book."

"You paid twenty-five cents too much."

Giovanni never understood the concept of using a book to meet someone. He preferred to just let it happen naturally. Whenever it happened. Why try to force things? Hell, he would know better than anyone that you shouldn't force things. All that pressure from his mother to produce grandchildren got him into a relationship that wasn't even healthy, let alone satisfying. No, Patricia wasn't a terrible woman. But they had different goals and needs. And that was a recipe for disaster. And not just any disaster. Take a hurricane and throw in an earthquake and a few hundred tornadoes. *That* type of disaster.

Giovanni took another sip. "You think you can apply a few things that you read in a book to meet the girl of your dreams?"

"Pretty much, yeah," said Stevie.

"You wish it was that easy."

Danny perked up in his chair. "Hey, you know who's got it easy? Porcupines."

Giovanni sighed. "I'm not sure I want to hear this."

Danny ignored him. "When a male porcupine wants to

get freaky with a female porcupine he just pisses on her."

"Right."

"It's true. He just whips out his porcupine penis and takes a serious wiz all over Miss Porcupine U.S.A. Then if the female is interested they have porcupine sex right there. Doesn't matter where they are. Downtown. Yosemite. Levi's Stadium."

"She must really stink," said Stevie.

Giovanni ground his teeth. "Love stinks."

"Love Stinks!" said Danny. "That was performed by the J. Geils Band. 1979."

"Stick a sock in it, Ryan Seacrest," said Stevie.

Giovanni laughed.

He was right earlier. It was good to try to get back to the normal things. Like hanging out with two guys who typically drove him nuts. He'd been friends with Danny and Stevie since elementary school and he loved them as if they were his brothers.

Two hours later and with plenty of coffee and sweets under their belts, Giovanni and the boys left Dolce Spazio.

He knew it would only be a matter of seconds before Stevie suggested they go crash the bachelorette party.

Wasn't going to happen.

*****

As they approached the Los Gatos Brewing Company

Stevie pointed to the front door. "Just a few minutes, Giovanni. We can just go in, say hello to the ladies, and be out of there in no time."

So predictable.

Giovanni kept walking. "No."

He forced himself to look straight ahead as he passed by the place. He knew if he saw Natalie in one the windows he would be tempted.

"Hey!" said Stevie, grabbing Giovanni's arm and stopping him in his tracks. "Look at that group of women! And the bride with that tiara on her head." Stevie squeezed Giovanni's arm a few times. "That's Federico's granddaughter? Damn, she's smokin' hot!"

Giovanni couldn't control his body. It turned on its own toward the window where Natalie was. She was looking as beautiful as ever, surrounded by a large group of women. They were all laughing and talking and drinking.

She looked like an angel.

Natalie turned suddenly and met eyes with Giovanni through the window. He felt his pulse pounding in his neck. Although he didn't hear her, he could see she screamed. Then she pointed directly at Giovanni. All of the other women turned and looked outside to the sidewalk where the guys were standing.

"A buffet of beautiful women," said Stevie. "Let's eat."

"No," said Giovanni.

Natalie waved Giovanni inside. His heart sped up even

more—now he could feel the pounding in his temples.

"Dude!" said Stevie. "We just got the green light!"

Not good.

Giovanni didn't even really remember how it happened, but seconds later he was inside the place with the guys, surrounded by women. Natalie was going on and on about his custom guitars with her matron of honor, Rebecca.

"And he makes the guitars with his hands!" she said, appearing to be drunk.

"How many?" asked one of the bridesmaids, also appearing a little tipsy.

Giovanni held up his hands. "I have two. Just like everyone else."

Natalie laughed as though he'd told the funniest joke in the world. "Oh my God! Isn't he so funny?" She held one of Giovanni's hands up for display. "And did I tell you he makes them with his hands?"

Rebecca pried Giovanni's hand out of Natalie's and cleared her throat. "Yes, that was the second time you mentioned that."

Natalie snagged his hand back and rubbed her cheek with it. "They're really soft."

"I've got soft hands too," said Stevie. "Anyone want to touch them?"

The women ignored Stevie, obviously more interested in the show Natalie was putting on.

She smelled Giovanni's hand. "What kind of lotion do

you use? I could smell this all day long. Yummy!"

Giovanni didn't know how to respond. "Well..."

Natalie showed Giovanni's hand to the other women, practically ripping his arm out of his socket. "And you think these hands are nice? Ha! You should see the guy without clothes! H-O-T baby, baby, baby!"

Yeah. Definitely drunk.

Stevie stared at Giovanni, hands on hips. "Is there something you'd like to tell us?"

Giovanni shrugged. "Not really."

Rebecca stepped forward and took Natalie's hand again. "Okay! Looks like this is going to be an early night—*someone* needs to be cut off. Show of hands, who's drunk?"

Ten hands went up.

Rebecca sighed. "Oh boy. We're going to have to call a few taxis."

"We can take Natalie home if you want," said Giovanni. "She lives next door to me."

"Yes!" said Natalie. "Giovanni can take me. Take me, baby!" She laughed uncontrollably and then snorted.

Rebecca placed her hand over Natalie's mouth. "That's probably not a good idea."

Giovanni shrugged. "We haven't had anything to drink."

Natalie tried to speak but the words were garbled since Rebecca's hand was still covering her mouth. Rebecca removed her hand. "How can we help you?"

"I was trying to say that....uh...what was I trying to say?

Oh, that's right! Giovanni is a man."

Rebecca nodded. "You're very observant, but that's not going to get you home."

"Yes it is! He is a man and I am a woman. Two consenting adults who live next to each other. Isn't that convenient? That's why it's so easy for me to see him walking around in his sexy underwear! It makes perfect sense and sensibility that he drives me home."

"Sense and sensibility? Is that right?"

"Yes! He's not like anything *gross* like a serial killer. Ooh, a bowl of cereal sounds good. Or yummy waffles at Southern Kitchen!"

"*You* are going home."

"There's no place like home. Ha! Wait, what was I talking about earlier? Oh, oh! Have you seen Giovanni's hands?"

Rebecca laughed. "Oh my God. Yes, I've seen them. Okay, Mr. Giovanni, she made absolutely no sense whatsoever yet she convinced me that you are the man for the job. You're in charge of getting the bride home safe and sound."

"No problem."

At least he *hoped* it wouldn't be a problem. You never know what can happen when alcohol is involved.

Chapter Eight

Natalie had fallen asleep immediately on Giovanni's shoulder after she got in the car. He'd ordered Stevie and Danny to be quiet on the drive home and it was the most peace he'd had with those two since he met them in elementary school. But now it was time to wake the princess up and get her inside the house.

Stevie pulled in Giovanni's driveway.

Giovanni let out a deep breath. "Crap."

"What?" said Danny.

He pointed to the front door where two people were waiting. "Look."

Giovanni's parents.

"Shit," said Danny.

"Danny, help me get her out."

Danny got out and ran around to the other side to open the back door.

Giovanni lifted Natalie's head gently from his shoulder. "Let's go, Sleeping Beauty." He grabbed her purse from the floor of the car and slid Natalie out, with Danny's help.

She opened her eyes and came to life. "Waffles with warm syrup."

Giovanni smiled. "I love waffles."

Eleonora rushed to the car, followed closely by Alfonso. "What in the…where did you get this woman from? Did you find her?"

"Yes, Mom. I found her. Right next to a couple of pennies on the ground. What kind of a ridiculous question is that?"

"Mom?" said Natalie. "This is your mother, Giovanni? Oh, how cuuuuuuute. You have a mother, I forgot! Hey, please don't call your son names. He's a genius!"

Eleonora ignored Natalie and spoke directly to Giovanni. "Well, at least you know each other and you're trying to find another suitable mate. Good. Time is ticking. Is she fertile?"

"As fertile as a rabbit!" said Natalie.

"You need to marry this girl before she gets away like the others."

Natalie ran her fingers through Giovanni's hair. "Yes, let's get married!"

Giovanni removed her hand. "I'm not going to marry you."

Eleonora poked Giovanni in the chest. "How many times do I have to tell you to quit being a pussy?"

"Eleonora, please," said Alfonso.

"Go to the car, Alfie, before I castrate you."

Alfonso walked to the car with his head down. Giovanni admired his father for putting up with his mother for all these years. Alfonso was probably the most discreet and quiet man Giovanni knew. Just the opposite of Eleonora.

"Wait, wait, wait, wait, wait," said Natalie. "Your mother called you a pussy!" She stood up semi-straight and pushed herself out of the arms of Giovanni. She wobbled, trying to focus on Eleonora. "I ought to arrest you for public bitchiness!"

"There's no such thing."

Natalie gave Eleonora the stink eye. "Yeah? Well, you just wait for the next election. I'll make sure it's on the ballot. How do you like *them* apples?" She poked Eleonora in the chest. "Huh? How do you like them?"

"Ha!" said Stevie. "I like this woman and I'd pay top dollar to see a cat fight."

"Everyone, please leave," said Giovanni.

"Okay," said Natalie, trying to wobble away.

Giovanni grabbed her and held on. "Not you. I'm taking you inside."

She made a pouty face. "Why don't you want to marry me?"

Eleonora stood there with her hands on her hips. "Yes, Giovanni Roma. Why don't you want to marry this beautiful *fertile* woman? There's an open offer on the table. Take it."

"Like the last one? Look how well that worked! This is not one of your real estate transactions. Life doesn't work that way."

"I want grandchildren!"

Natalie held her hand up. "I'm a fertile rabbit! Will you marry me? Me-oooooooow."

Alfonso rolled down the window of the car. "Please, Eleonora, let's go."

Eleonora pointed her finger at Alfonso and scowled. "Castration, Alfie!"

Alfonso sighed and rolled the window back up.

"Everyone," said Giovanni. "Leave. Now."

Eleonora sighed and walked to her car. "This is not over!"

"Believe me, I know!" said Giovanni.

He held on to Natalie's side and walked her to the front door. He didn't look back as he heard the cars leaving.

He was going to knock on the door but remembered that Federico was at his book club meeting. "I need to get your keys out of your purse. You have keys, right?"

"Of course! They're the ones that look like…keys!"

Giovanni laughed. "Good to know."

He kept her upright with one arm and used his free hand to reach into the purse to grab the keys. He didn't like to see her this way but it felt good to help her. Heck, it felt good to hold her too.

He got her in the house and into the guest bedroom. The room smelled like her. Fresh. Pretty. He liked that smell. A lot. He flicked on the light and led her toward the queen-sized bed.

"Beddy bye time!" She collapsed on the bed facedown.

Giovanni rolled her over, careful not to cop an accidental feel. He gently slid her shoes off. Cute feet with pink toenails. He pulled the comforter from one side of the bed and slid it over the top of her so she was covered. Then he tucked it in along the side of her body, from her feet all the way up to her neck.

"So this is what a burrito feels like. I like this, I'm very comfy. You're very sweet, Giovanni Roma. Are you sure you don't want to marry me?"

She looked like an angel lying there. Sure, a drunk angel, but still. And he loved her jasmine smell.

If she wasn't engaged and drunk maybe he would have taken her up on the offer. She was a thousand times more down-to-earth than the women from his last two failed relationships.

But no. It wasn't going to happen, obviously.

She was drunk. And even more importantly, she was engaged.

He tucked her in a little more and forced a smile. "*You* are already getting married. To someone else."

She lost her smile. "Well…you're more fun!"

She untucked her arms from the comforter, caught Giovanni by the back of the neck, pulled him down, and kissed him on the lips. A lingering kiss.

Then she collapsed back down to the bed and started snoring.

Giovanni brushed the hair away from her face. "You are one amazing woman, Natalie. Amazing. Too bad your fiancé doesn't realize what he's got."

Maybe that's why she drank so much.

*****

The next morning, Natalie sat on the back porch with a cup of coffee watching the hummingbirds drink from the red feeder. The hangover was a bitch. The pounding in her head only just started to go away and Federico's peaceful backyard was helping. She took a deep breath and enjoyed the morning air. Another sip of coffee and her phone rang. So much for peace and quiet.

She picked up her phone and checked the caller ID.

Rebecca.

Although she didn't feel like talking, Natalie didn't remember much about last night so Rebecca could fill her in. Hopefully she didn't make a fool of herself.

She answered. "Please tell me I didn't dance on the tables last night or anything like that."

Rebecca laughed. "No, no. Nothing like that."

"Thank God."

"It was much worse."

Fudge! "Tell me. What happened?"

"Sorry to be the bearer of bad news."

Natalie took another sip of coffee. "Please don't tell me that. I don't even remember how I got home."

"Ahhh. Well, that ride was courtesy of Prince Charming with the amazing hands."

What the hell was she talking about? And who the hell was

Prince Charming?

"Okay, I guess you were more trashed than I thought. You don't remember seeing Giovanni last night?"

"Giovanni?" Natalie hesitated and tried to focus on the details of last night. "Uh…."

"So then you definitely don't remember being all googly-eyed over him and touching his hands?"

"Touching his—"

"You were rubbing your face with his hands. You may have even had an orgasm."

"Very funny."

"I'm serious! The way you were going on, I thought you were going to drop his hands a little bit lower."

"Shit. I can't believe I—" Natalie watched as Precious approached her in the yard, wagging her tail. "Precious?"

What was the dog doing there?

"No, it's me, Rebecca. Are you still drunk?"

"No, I'm not still drunk. Giovanni's dog Precious is in our yard."

"You know what that means, right?"

"No."

"Prince Charming won't be far behind her."

Natalie whipped her head toward the fence to see if Giovanni was coming in. Thank God, no. She knew she looked like hell so she didn't want to be seen. And after last night's performance, maybe she needed to hide from him for the rest of her life.

"Arf!"

"No, Precious, don't do that," she whispered. "We don't want Giovanni to know you're here."

"Arf! Arf!"

"Okay, Rebecca, I need to go. Chat with you later."

Natalie disconnected. Precious continued to bark.

"Shhh!" She petted her and tried to calm her down. Did she want to play? Maybe she was hungry.

"Arf!"

"Precious?" came a yell from the other side of the fence. "Where are you? Come here, girl!"

Fudge!

Natalie kept her head down and snuck behind the barbecue. Precious followed her and Natalie tried to push her away. Not gonna happen.

The dog began to lick Natalie's fingers and she giggled. "Precious, that tickles. Don't do that. And shoo! Giovanni is coming and I look like death!"

"Precious?" yelled Giovanni.

"Arf!"

"Are you over in Federico's yard? Ah, the gate is open—that would explain it."

Natalie peeked toward the fence and saw Giovanni approaching—she crouched down even further. How mature. A grown woman, a cop, hiding behind a barbecue. Now if only Precious would move in his direction maybe he wouldn't catch her acting like a five-year old.

"Come here," said Giovanni. "What are you doing over here? I—"

You *what?* What was he doing?

Natalie didn't want to peek because she knew Giovanni was only a few feet away. But what happened? Why did he stop talking? The curiosity was driving her mad. She couldn't hear him moving, breathing, nothing. The only sound was a distant lawn mower. Did Giovanni and Precious just disappear?

"You shouldn't be over here," said Giovanni. "I don't think Federico wants poop in his yard and Natalie is probably sleeping after what she did last night. We don't want to wake up Sleeping Beauty, do we?"

"Arf!"

Sleeping Beauty?

Did he really think she was beautiful or was that sarcasm? Natalie wanted to see his facial expression.

"Okay, it wouldn't be so bad to see Natalie, but she's probably passed out where I left her, still tucked in her beautiful bed under her purple comforter. All cozy. Snoring like a hippopotamus."

Hold up. Wait a minute. Back up! Forget about the hippopotamus comment—I've been called worse. What did he say before that? She's passed out where I left her?

Had he been in her bedroom? Did he tuck her in? Obviously he did; he knew the color of her comforter. Not being able to remember what happened last night was enough to almost make her break out in hives. But the thought of him tucking her in sounded nice too.

Ahhh!

She felt so conflicted.

"You need to quit licking my face like that, Precious. I am not that kind of guy."

Too bad.

"Okay, let's go," said Giovanni.

Natalie heard the crunch of leaves on the grass moving farther and farther away, followed by the sound of the gate closing. She waited until she heard them go inside Giovanni's house and close the side door before she stood up and went inside. At least he didn't see her.

She went inside to get ready for her shift. Having to work the day after a bachelorette party was certainly poor planning on her part but maybe she would feel better once she got moving and the blood was circulating.

She felt guilty, though. She was going to be getting married soon and her thoughts were not on the groom. Jacks didn't call last night to check in on her and still hadn't called this morning. This was the first time she'd thought of him this morning because her thoughts were on another man.

Giovanni.

Not good.

Chapter Nine

Giovanni laced up his shoes and left the house for an afternoon walk with Precious. He had to admit he was enjoying the dog's company. She was cute and funny. And she distracted him when he didn't want to think about his debacle of a love life and his poor choice of women.

Hopefully he could put in a few miles before getting back to work on James' guitar.

After the first mile Precious was still right by his side, keeping pace with Giovanni.

What a cool companion!

He turned the corner and spotted a cop car parked in front of Pizza My Heart. His heart rate sped up. Was it Natalie? He glanced inside the open window of the cop car as he passed it.

It was a male cop. Nice try.

He shouldn't be thinking about Natalie anyway. Although he couldn't help but smile when he thought of her hiding behind the barbecue. He really did want to say something but figured she was embarrassed about last night.

Giovanni made a left on Main Street and passed Le Boulanger and the Los Gatos Coffee Roasting Company.

Precious coughed a few times and pulled toward the water bowl sitting on the sidewalk directly in front of Village House of Books.

Hairball?

No, wait—hairballs were for cats. She took a few sips of the water and looked content—smiling up at Giovanni.

He reached down to pet her on the head. "Better?"

She licked his hand.

I guess that's a yes!

Giovanni crossed the bridge over Highway 17 and stopped again.

This time for Natalie.

She was writing a ticket for a motorcycle parked on the sidewalk. He couldn't pass up the opportunity to say something, but needed to think of something to say.

"Arf!"

Great. So much for waiting for the right moment.

Natalie turned around and looked down at Precious. Her eyes traveled from the dog right up Giovanni's legs, pausing on his chest, then continued to his face, where he was greeted with what seemed to be a forced smile. Yeah. She was probably embarrassed.

But he was pretty sure she was checking him out!

Yeah. In my dreams.

Precious pulled in her direction—obviously recognizing Natalie—and Giovanni moved with her until he was face to face with Natalie.

"I know you've been trying to avoid me," he said.

"I don't know what you're talking about."

She placed her hands on her hips and struck what she probably thought was an intimidating pose. Ha! That wasn't going to work on him anymore. He was getting to know her pretty well.

Giovanni smiled. "No barbecues to hide behind downtown."

Natalie opened her mouth then closed it.

"What? You really didn't think I could see you?"

She shrugged. "Okay, you got me."

"You got that right."

"I was embarrassed."

Giovanni nodded. "I figured as much with your impression of *Crouching Tiger, Hidden Dragon*. Honestly…I probably wouldn't have noticed if it wasn't for your cup of coffee and slippers on the deck and the fact that the barbecue had brown hair growing out of the back."

"That's the last time I play hide and seek with you."

Giovanni laughed. "You've recovered then? I'm surprised you're actually working today."

Natalie nodded. "Yeah. Don't know what I was thinking. Physically, I'm doing better than expected. Mentally, not so much. I certainly wasn't on my best behavior." She avoided eye contact with Giovanni. "My friend Rebecca told me I did a few…embarrassing things. One of them involved your hands or something like that."

He wasn't going to complain about how many times she grabbed him. Her hands were soft. So were her lips.

Giovanni grinned. "And those are just the things you did when Rebecca was around. Imagine how crazy you got when you and I were alone."

She looked up and wrinkled her nose. "Do I want to know?"

"You probably wouldn't believe it."

"Give me a sample. At least so I know if I should move to a different city and change my name."

"Okay, which do you want to know first? The part where you proposed to me in front of my parents or the part where you kissed me on the bed?"

Giovanni couldn't identify the color of Natalie's face. If he were to make up a color he would say it was shocked tomato.

"Please tell me you're joking," she said.

"I'm sorry, I just can't do that. The last time I lied you threatened to arrest me."

She stood there in silence.

"You've helped me out when I was about to break the law on a couple of occasions, but I actually helped you too."

"How?" she asked.

"Being married to two people is against the law so I respectfully declined your proposal."

"How noble of you."

She bit her lower lip and fidgeted with her holster.

Poor girl. He didn't want her to suffer so he thought he'd

help her out and change the subject. "What time do you get off today?"

"Five." She cocked her head to the side. "Why? Looking for more ways to embarrass me?"

"No. It's just—"

Giovanni felt his heart rate speed up. He was thinking of asking her out. Not on a date, really. Just to get together.

Shit.

His heart was going to explode from his chest, he was sure of it. What would he gain from asking her out? The woman was getting married!

Just do it, bozo.

"You doing anything after? You can join the two of us on a hike, if you want. It's not very hot and Precious would enjoy it, I think."

"You and Precious?"

Giovanni nodded.

"Weren't you just walking?"

"Yeah, just a little bit. I think we're going to head back because I'm getting hungry all of a sudden."

"Arf!"

"I guess she's hungry too—isn't that right?"

"Arf!"

"I thought so."

Natalie pointed to her squad car. "I better get back to work. I don't know about the hike. It may not be the best idea."

"That's a good point. Exercise can kill you, just like stationary cars." Giovanni smiled and she matched it. Damn, he was sure they had a connection. "Okay, look, if you want to join us, excellent. If not, that's okay too." He pointed just past Natalie on the right. "We'll be at the bottom of St. Joseph's Hill at six on the nose. And if you're nice I may just tell you what else you did last night."

"There was more?"

"I'm sorry, I'm not able to divulge that information at this time. Six o'clock."

She nodded. "Okay."

Giovanni and Precious turned around and headed back home. Natalie was hard to read—he wasn't sure if she was going to join them. But he hoped she would.

Giovanni ran up his driveway and stopped at the door with Precious. He sat on the step of the front porch to take off his shoes as Precious plopped down next to him. A few seconds later he heard the rumble of a car and watched as a red Ferrari pulled up directly in front of his house. The last person in the world he expected to be in that car got out.

Patricia.

She looked different. Slim, as usual, but new clothes and hairstyle. She walked confidently toward Giovanni in a charcoal tight skirt below her knees, a white shirt, and a light jacket matching her skirt. Giovanni could hear the sound of her heels and her long necklaces as she approached. Her blond hair was up in a high bun.

Giovanni pointed to the Ferrari. "New car?"

She took off her sunglasses. "A friend's."

Right. Must be the guy from the French restaurant. Not gonna go there.

Her eyes were covered with different layers of makeup. Her eyelashes seemed much longer than before. Did she get extensions?

She pointed to Precious. "Cute dog. Yours?"

"Just dog sitting."

"I didn't know you liked dogs."

Yeah. There were obviously a lot of things Patricia didn't know about him. But who was he to talk? She was like a stranger to him.

Patricia reached down to pet Precious and the dog snapped at her. It wasn't easy, but Giovanni was able to hold in the laughter. The dog seemed to be a good judge of character.

She pointed toward the house. "I just came by to pick up the things I had here."

Shit.

Giovanni was not looking forward to this conversation. He didn't answer.

"I can grab everything real quick if you don't mind."

"Yeah. Well, about that. I kind of…donated everything to charity."

She stared at him. "My stuff?

He nodded.

"My clothes, my shoes, my purses? Everything?"

He nodded again.

Her body shook a little and her breathing became heavy. Convulsions? Was she going to pass out? She closed her eyes and took a couple of deep breaths and let them out slowly. She looked slightly psychotic. He needed to watch out or she may do something crazy like—

"You asshole!" Patricia removed one of her shoes and threw it at Giovanni. It smacked him right in the head.

Glad it wasn't with the heel!

"Arf! Arf! Arf!"

Giovanni rubbed his head and shielded Precious so she wouldn't get hurt. "Watch it. You're going to break something!"

Patricia removed the other shoe and Giovanni dodged it. It bounced off the front door.

With Precious under his arm Giovanni ran and picked up both shoes. "Thank you! More to donate!"

"Those are Prada! I should break your neck! Do you know how much that stuff is worth?"

"Not a clue. You got those at Marshalls, right?"

"Ahhhhhhh!" She held up her middle finger to Giovanni and walked back to the Ferrari barefoot.

"Arf! Arf! Arf!"

Giovanni scratched Precious on the head to calm her down. "It's okay, girl. She's gone."

Patricia pulled out her cell phone before she got in the car and made a call. "Meet me at Nordstrom's in ten minutes. Time for a shopping spree and you're treating." She disconnected the call, gave Giovanni the evil eye, got in the car, and drove away.

He sighed and went inside with Precious. It was odd seeing her.

Very odd.

If there was any connection it was gone for sure. He wondered if they ever had one. She looked like she found a sugar daddy and he was okay with that. He had no hard feelings. He wished her the best.

He took a quick shower and headed to his mom's house with Precious. Eleonora said she had something for him and that he had to come by today before it expired. He had no idea what it was but he planned to be at her house at five. That would give him an hour before the hike.

*****

As he pulled up to the front of his parents' house he saw a car parked in his usual spot in the driveway. A bright red Smart car. Those cars always made Giovanni smile— they reminded him of a carnival ride. Tiny and cute. Quite opposite of his mom's car. If you wanted to call it a car. She drove a Hummer. But it made sense since she needed a place for her giant balls.

His dad stood there with the front door open and a face

longer than Florida. "Hi son."

They hugged and Alfonso closed the door behind them.

His dad looked down at Precious. "Cute dog. What's her name?"

"Precious."

He nodded. "You sure you want to bring that thing in here? You know what's going to happen when your mother sees her."

"She'll just have to deal with it."

Giovanni heard his mom talking with another woman in the other room. "Oh no."

His dad put his arm around Giovanni and whispered. "Just remember, I had nothing to do with this one either. If you ever decide to kill your mother I will be your alibi. I promise."

Giovanni knew his dad was joking but he didn't like the sound of things. His poor dad, neutered by his mother. And he knew that face. It meant his mother was up to no good.

Giovanni could hear the two talking in the family room. He decided he wanted no part of it. He slowly started backing up toward the door.

Alfonso grabbed him by the arm. "Nice try. She already knows you're here, so if you don't want to start World War III you'll just go in there and get this over with."

Giovanni knew what was going on. His mother was trying to set him up with another woman. A woman who was pre-screened to be certain that she wanted lots of babies. They'd been through this before and it was about as enjoyable as a kick to the head.

He took a deep breath and politely smiled as he entered the family room, waiting for his mother to start the show. He had to admit, as annoying as it was, his mother was a damn good actress.

"Hi son!" she said, moving to him and kissing him on the cheek. The last time she kissed him on the cheek was when she set him up on a blind date with Patricia. And look how that turned out.

Eleonora glanced down at Precious who was sniffing her leg. "What is this thing doing in my house?"

"Her name is Precious and I'm watching her for a friend."

"It has hair."

"Most dogs do."

"Please put her in the backyard."

Giovanni hesitated, but didn't want to argue with her so he slid open the sliding glass door and let Precious outside. The dog looked happy and started exploring the back yard. She would be okay back there for a little while.

Giovanni knew his mother would be pissed if he didn't play along with her game and he wasn't in the mood to play with fire.

"Hi Mom." He pretended to inspect her hair. "Did you do something different with your hair? I *love* it."

He hated playing this game.

Giovanni's dad hovered quietly in the background,

pretending to organize something.

Eleonora palmed both of her cheeks and pretended to be surprised. "That's my son, always so sweet." Then she went in for another kiss on the cheek! "Son, I want to introduce you to a very special woman I know from my Pilates class—her name is…Choo."

"Bless you, Mother."

His mother pursed her lips and mouthed the word *no*. Then she said, "*Choo*, this is my son, Giovanni."

Oh.

Her name was Choo.

As in *choo choo* train.

As in *chew* before you swallow.

As in *Chew*bacca.

"Son?"

Shit. There were words spoken and Giovanni missed them. He hated when that happened. His mind was still on the movie *Star Wars*.

"Yes?"

"Choo is waiting to hug you."

"Oh"

Giovanni glanced at Choo. She was as short as his mother but half her weight. Her straight black hair rested on her shoulders and her tiny nose was flaring. She looked excited.

A little too much.

Choo held both of her arms wide open and smiled. "Come to mama."

Mama?

She snapped her finger and pointed to the floor in front of her. "Now! Quit being so shy! Your mother told me you were a hugger. Show me what you've got."

Giovanni moved in for the hug and Choo squeezed him tight with both hands. She applied pressure to his lower back and rolled her fists in an upward motion from his waist up to his neck. He now knew what it was like to be a tube of toothpaste while someone tries to squeeze the last bit out.

She inhaled before she released him. "And you smell good enough to eat!"

Somebody help me.

Eleonora squealed like a guinea pig. "You and Choo have so much in common!"

Giovanni raised an eyebrow. "Like what?"

"*You* build guitars and *she* makes origami."

He scratched his head. "Okay. And…how is that the same?"

"You both make things with your hands!"

"Yes!" said Choo, "And also you have lots of money. And I *like* lots of money!"

Eleonora covered her face with her hand.

"Is that what my mom told you?"

"Yes! Happy! Happy!"

Choo screamed with delight and moved in for another hug-massage-toothpaste-tube squeeze.

This time he was pretty sure he felt a couple of bones

crack.

Hopefully there wasn't permanent damage.

"Mom, I'd really love to stay but I'm meeting someone for a hike and have to get going."

Eleonora gave him a serious look and pursed her lips. "That's fine, dear. Let's get down to business then."

"Business?"

Choo grabbed a briefcase from the floor and opened it. "I'm in there like swimwear." She sorted through some papers and handed the first one to Giovanni. "Here's my resume."

Giovanni eyed the resume.

Someone shoot me. Is she applying to be my wife?

Choo handed him three more pieces of paper that were stapled together. "This is my medical exam report." She pointed to the top. "As you can see it was dated just yesterday. I know the doctor so he rushed them for me! You won't have to worry about me dying on you—I am *very* healthy. This here shows my thyroid, estrogen, and hormone levels. As you can see I'm ready to go!"

Eleonora lit up. "Choo has five brothers and each of her parents has five brothers. Go testosterone!"

"Oh!" continued Choo. She rustled through her papers. "Where is it? Where is it? Here!" She found a piece of paper with an image on it. "I had an ultrasound and *this* is a picture of my uterus! Cherry condition, right?"

Giovanni sighed. "Just like my friend's '58 Cadillac."

Choo laughed uncontrollably.

Giovanni couldn't take it anymore. He stacked her papers together neatly and forced a smile. "Thank you. I need to run now."

"Wonderful! I look forward to hearing from you. Let me know if you need references from men or anything like that."

"Of course."

She went in for the kill one more time and squeezed the last bit of toothpaste out of Giovanni. He let Precious back in from the backyard, hugged his father like normal people hug, and walked out the door.

Hopefully Natalie would show up for the hike.

He was in the mood to hang out with a normal person.

Chapter Ten

Natalie waited for Giovanni at the bottom of St. Joseph's Hill and wondered what it was about that guy that made her hands sweat. She felt different when she was around him— that was for sure. She liked his company and the way he looked at her too. But this was not a date. She was engaged and Giovanni was a friend—a new friend whose company she would enjoy. That's all.

Jacks had called in the afternoon and left her a message saying he would have to work late on an important case against some mafia guy. What else was new? They all seemed to be the most important cases of his career. Luckily, when Jacks hadn't been around she'd been able to enjoy quality time with Federico—their meals together, talking, and sharing memories.

She did feel a tad bit of guilt for two reasons. One, she called Jacks back to say she was going on a hike but she failed to mention one important detail. That she was going with Giovanni.

And two, she found herself nervously changing her shorts three times before she left the house.

But it was time to try to put all of that out of her head.

She was excited to be out in nature and was ready to enjoy a hike with Giovanni.

She bent down to retie her shoelaces and got a lick on the face.

Precious.

She petted the dog on the head and stood up to greet Giovanni. "Hi."

"Hi. Glad you could make it."

She noticed his eyes briefly wander down to her legs before quickly jumping back up to meet her gaze. She obviously had chosen the right shorts to wear.

"I have ulterior motives," said Natalie. "I need to find out everything I did last night and then make a decision if I am going to go into hiding or leave the country."

Giovanni laughed. "It wasn't that bad."

"No?"

"Okay, maybe it was." He gestured with his hand toward the trail to start walking.

She wasn't sure what it was about him, but she felt so comfortable in Giovanni's presence. He just seemed so down to earth and sincere. From what she could tell—and from what Federico told her—it really didn't make any sense why the woman left him.

Maybe she would find out the reason soon.

They walked a little bit without speaking and she was okay with that. She admired the view of the trees, the creek, and the man hiking directly in front of her. But curiosity got the best of her.

"I would like to know something."

Giovanni stopped and turned around. "No, I didn't take a peek at your goodies when I tucked you in bed."

"I wasn't going to ask you that!"

He chuckled. "Sorry. Please continue."

She analyzed him and figured out he was kidding. Okay, she needed to loosen up.

She decided to try again. "Why do you think she didn't show up to the church?"

"Who?"

She stopped, her hands on her hips. "Who? What do you mean who?"

"I mean which one. I was jilted twice."

"Oh…"

There's got to be something wrong with this guy. That must mean that he is the problem. Two times? That can't be a coincidence.

"It was just a coincidence. They are completely different women and completely unrelated."

"Maybe it's not them, it's you."

Oops. Hopefully that wasn't too harsh.

Precious stopped by the creek and drank some water. Giovanni seemed lost, staring in the water for a few moments. Definitely too harsh.

Fudge!

Looked like the foot had found the mouth again.

Natalie decided to switch gears. "How long are you

watching Precious?"

"Two weeks. The owner—Beatrice is her name—went on a cruise."

Precious finished drinking half the water in the creek and they continued the hike, going up a little bit of a slope. And there was Giovanni's nice butt again, on display for her pleasure.

Thank you!

"I hope you're not checking out my ass," said Giovanni.

"What? Dream on!"

A little bit of that guilt came back.

Focus!

"I must say," said Giovanni. "I'm quite surprised you gave up on discussing my failed relationships."

"Oh, I didn't give up."

"No?"

"I'm just pacing myself so I don't overwhelm you."

"Very smart. What about you?"

"What about me?"

He shrugged. "You know, getting married and all that jazz."

"Yeah."

"Yeah? You are getting ready for the biggest day of your life and all you can say is 'yeah'?"

"What do you want me to say?"

"I don't know. I guess I just expected a little more excitement from someone I've gotten to first base with."

Natalie pushed Giovanni in the back. He let go of the leash and slipped on some leaves. He slid down the slope, but was able to stop the slide by latching on to a bush with this hand.

Shit. I didn't mean to push him that hard. Really.

"Oops. Are you okay?"

*****

Giovanni had to admit the girl had some spunk. He shouldn't be surprised considering she was a cop. She could probably kick his ass any day of the week. He would have to seriously consider his word choices before letting them exit his mouth in the future. He almost laughed, but held it in for fear of getting pushed again. Maybe this time off a cliff.

He got up and wiped off his shirt and shorts then pointed back to the plant. "I have a sneaking suspicion you just pushed me into poison oak."

"Nooooo." She leaned over to try to get a better look. "I can't tell from here. But just to be safe, you should wash well with mild soap and lukewarm water when you get back."

Giovanni stared at his hand. "Okay."

Natalie took a step, slid on the dirt, and lost her balance. Giovanni reached out and grabbed her, catching her before she fell over. He pulled her up and their bodies were now touching.

She looked down at her hand. "I guess I may need to wash

too."

"Uh huh."

Jasmine.

She smelled even better than when he tucked her in that night. And now she was looking up into his eyes, neither one saying a word. He felt movement in his shorts and jumped back, hopefully before she noticed.

"What?" she said.

No way he was going to tell her the truth. She pushed him down a hill just because he mentioned an innocent kiss. A kiss *she* initiated! That's what he got for telling the truth? He didn't want to imagine what the crazy, sexy cop would do if he mentioned he was sporting a hard-on for her.

"Nothing," he said. "I thought I saw a bee."

"A bee…" she said, eying his shorts. "Uh huh."

So much for her not knowing.

"Shall we continue?" he asked, not waiting for an answer and heading—almost running—up the hill. Fortunately Precious was just as motivated as he was.

"Not a bad idea. And maybe this would be a good time to get back to our conversation regarding your failed relationships."

"I thought maybe you were distracted and forgot."

"Forgot?" said Natalie. "Right. I'm a woman, remember?"

Oh, I remember alright!

"Good point," said Giovanni. "In that case, it would be a thrill to talk about my relationships with you. What would you like to know?"

"Simple. What happened?"

Simple? Ha! He wished he knew what happened. Maybe she could help him figure it out.

He shrugged. "I don't know…"

"Okay, quit beating around the bush and tell me."

"Fine." He stopped and turned back. "But let's switch places—you walk in front of me. Precious is starting to slow down and I think she will be more motivated if she has someone to follow."

Natalie had a suspicious look on her face.

What did I do?

Oh. Maybe she thought he wanted her in front so he could check out her ass. It honestly hadn't crossed his mind. Until now.

Yup, *now* he was thinking of her ass.

She passed him and trekked upward. "Shall we continue?"

"Absolutely."

He stared at the back of her purple tank top and it only took a few seconds before his gaze started to drop.

Shit.

That was a beautiful ass.

Wow.

No. Double wow.

How was he supposed to focus on anything now? He hadn't planned on looking, but how could he not? Really, each cheek was perfectly positioned and her legs were absolutely edible. It was as though he was being hypnotized by them. He needed to stop looking there.

Stop it!

Okay, that didn't work.

Natalie stopped and turned around. Shit. He pulled his eyes off of her ass and raised them to meet her gaze. He was absolutely certain she caught him checking out her ass. He looked down at her foot that was tapping the ground.

Yup. She saw.

But that wasn't fair! Had she seen her own ass? Could she really blame him? Even a dead man would be checking out that ass! Now she was looking at his shorts again, obviously looking for clues. He dropped the hand that wasn't holding the dog leash down in front of his shorts to hide the evidence.

She shook her head. "Are you going to answer the question?"

"Of course," he said, thinking for a moment. "Uh…what was the question again?"

Another big sigh. "How did you meet your ex fiancée?"

"Oh, okay—that's an easy question. My mom set us up."

Natalie stopped and Giovanni ran into her back. She had to stop doing that.

She turned around and cocked her head to the side. "Your mom set you up?"

"That's what I said, yeah. Why do you say it like that?"

"I don't know. That sounds weird." She turned and

continued up the hill. "How long did you know her before you got engaged?"

"Three months." Giovanni ran into her back again. "You really need to stop doing that."

"I can't help it! I mean, what you said is very…telling."

"What? That we only knew each other for a short time so maybe we didn't *really* know each other at all? Big deal. I'm sure we could find thousands of cases that prove that theory wrong."

"Okay, you probably could. But three months? I think the odds are against you from the beginning. But let me ask you this: how long did you know your *first* fiancée before you got engaged?"

Maybe if he didn't answer she wouldn't notice.

He really didn't want to talk about her. That break up was much more devastating than the last one. In fact, this last one was a piece of cake compared to the first. He needed to distract her with something. Anything.

Giovanni pointed to the sky. "Look at those ducks! I love how they all fly in formation like fighter pilots. It's as if—"

"Nice try—I'm a cop. Remember? Not that I don't appreciate nature and animals, but I saw your diversion coming a mile away."

"You're good."

"Thank you. Answer the question."

"I'd be happy to. But only after I race you to the top."

Giovanni took off running with Precious following behind.

He could hear the footsteps pounding the dirt behind him, which surprised him. He thought for sure that he left her in the dust, but this woman was fast!

Just a few feet from the top and Giovanni felt the burn in his legs as that sexy cop passed him like he was a statue. How could that be? He ran track in high school and even played a few years of soccer. He was no slouch.

They came to a clearing and Natalie threw her arms in the air. "Yes!"

She broke into a little victory dance, if that's what you wanted to call it. It was like a mix of moves from Vanilla Ice, Michael Jackson, and Usher. She was all over the place.

Giovanni laughed and gestured toward the bench. "Okay, okay. You kicked my ass."

"It wasn't *that* bad. Well, okay, maybe it was."

She laughed as they both sat down. Precious laid underneath the bench, now panting a little. Giovanni opened up his water, poured some in his hand, and dropped his hand under the bench where the thirsty dog started licking.

Giovanni looked over to Natalie who was waiting. "I'm not ignoring you and I will answer you. Please stand by…"

"Of course." She reached under the bench and pet Precious who was drinking another serving from Giovanni's hand.

Giovanni wiped his hand on his shirt and said, "I knew my first fiancée two years before I asked her to marry me."

"Oh…"

"That's what I'm saying—they are two completely separate cases."

"But getting dumped on your wedding day two times in a row...*that* is not so random. What happened with the first one? Did you ever find out why she decided not to show up to your wedding?"

Giovanni nodded.

"And?"

He shrugged.

"Sorry. You don't have to talk about it."

"No, no, it's okay. I'll tell you." He let out a big breath. "I was head over heels for her and we had something very special, but—let's just say she didn't see eye-to-eye with my mom about certain things."

"Your mom caused your breakup?"

"My mom can be intense. *Too* intense. And she placed certain demands on Mandy that ended up being just too much. I really don't blame her for not showing up. But it broke my heart."

"What types of demands?"

"My mother is obsessed with having grandchildren. Always has been. When Mandy and I were together that's all my mom would talk about. She even wanted us to give her an exact date as to when she should expect the first baby. Down to the week."

"Oh God."

"But wait, it gets better! My mother wasn't going to be

happy if Mandy and I had a girl. It had to be a boy."

"You've got to be kidding me."

"She wanted a boy to carry on the family name after me. When she found out that Mandy had a long history of girls in her family she flipped out. She bought us books on how to make sure the baby was a boy. What to eat and what to drink every day. Lifestyles, sleeping patterns, thoughts. Even sexual positions. Can you believe that? My mom bought me a book on sexual positions!"

"Sorry, but it sounds like your mom belongs in the nut house." Natalie got up and stretched in front of Giovanni. Then she bent down to pet Precious who looked like she was almost asleep. "So the same thing happened with the second fiancée, then?"

"No. After what my mom did with Mandy, I told her I would disown her if she ever did it again. I have no idea why Patricia didn't want to marry me."

"Maybe you should ask her."

Giovanni nodded. He got up and stretched alongside Natalie. "Maybe, but does it matter now?"

"Sure it does. It will give you closure."

"Yeah, I guess so. I know one thing…Patricia changed. She wasn't like that at the beginning. Not so materialistic. We both wanted kids and—"

"Are you sure she changed? Or maybe you just didn't see her real personality? Sometimes when we start relationships we ignore the flaws because we want it to work, without realizing that the things that we are ignoring are the red flags that we should be paying attention to."

"Are you talking from experience?"

Hell yes. "No comment. But you should probably call her. To find out for sure."

"I think you're right. I'll give her a call. And hopefully she'll talk with me after what I did with her stuff. Thanks for the talk. It was nice."

Natalie pointed to herself. "I could be your psychologist!"

He laughed. "You probably could. Although I heard psychologists can't see their own problems. Make sure you pay attention to the red flags in your relationship!"

"Uh…of course. But right now I need to pay attention on the way back down."

Natalie was amazing. And Giovanni realized he was starting to have feelings for her.

Some would say these were just two friends getting together for a hike, but this felt like a date. He wasn't an idiot; he felt a connection with her and he was almost certain that she felt it too. And if she was so in love with Jacks, how come she hadn't mentioned him even once?

Giovanni pointed down the hill. "Okay, here we go."

"Arf!"

"See? Even Precious agrees."

"Arf!"

Natalie laughed and pointed to an older woman approaching with a poodle. "I have a feeling she was barking at the poodle and not answering you."

"Ha! I know Precious pretty well now and I know for a fact that she is *not* into poodles."

"Right." Precious pulled hard toward the poodle and sniffed it where dogs like to sniff. "Doesn't like poodles, huh? Right."

"She was being nice and saying hello. Didn't want to appear like a bitch to the general population."

Natalie laughed. He loved her laugh. It always ended with a little snort.

They headed down, Natalie first, and Giovanni only waited a few minutes before he decided to pry a little. "Now that you know my entire life's story, tell me about you and Jacks."

"What do you want to know?"

"How long have you known each other?"

She shrugged. "I'm not sure."

"I seem to remember that you are a woman and you remember *every*thing. Spill it."

"Six months."

"Seriously? Didn't you give me shit earlier for jumping into marriage too quickly with my second fiancé?"

She crinkled his nose. "I don't recall giving you shit."

"For a guy, my memory is not too bad and I recall you saying that the odds would be against me if I only knew her for three months before getting married."

"I don't recall. Anyway, six months is double the time you

date your ex."

"You're not in love, are you?"

She came to a halt and Giovanni ran into her back.

"If you were taller I would have a broken nose by now."

She turned around. "You calling me short?"

He hesitated. "No."

"You don't think I am in love with the man I am going to marry?"

"No. I don't. You don't even talk about him. And when I saw you two at the barbecue you barely talked to each other. I saw no connection whatsoever between the two of you. I'll tell you one thing…if you were my girl, I would show you how much I love you every single day. That guy doesn't know what he has. And why doesn't he kiss you?"

"He kisses me!"

"Well, if he does it's not enough. I didn't see him kiss you one time at the barbecue."

"Is that your new job? Kiss Counter?"

"Maybe it is. Kissing is good. Healthy. Enjoyable. Necessary."

"He's just preoccupied at work."

"If you say so. You can never be too busy to kiss. And you have amazing lips. They need to be kissed regularly."

"I—"

He reached down and plucked a purple flower from a bush on the side of the trail. He moved to Natalie.

She looked suspicious. "What are you doing?"

"Nothing. I think *this* belongs right *here*." He placed the flower in her hair just above her ear. "There. Since it's your favorite color, I just thought…"

Natalie looked like she wanted to say something but didn't speak. Maybe Giovanni's eyes were playing tricks on him, but it sure seemed like her eyes were watering. Was she crying?

"This is not right," she said. "Not right at all and it needs to stop."

She turned and headed down the hill.

Not another word the entire way down.

Not good.

He overdid it. Why did he have to stick that flower in her hair? It wasn't planned or anything. He just all of a sudden felt like sharing something with her. It was completely spontaneous. She drew that out of him so it was her fault!

At the bottom of the hill she gave Precious a pat on the head and reminded Giovanni to wash with mild soap and lukewarm water. She hadn't even left yet and Giovanni was already wondering when he could see her again. And also wondering what the hell he had got himself into. He liked her. A lot. And that most likely meant one thing on the horizon.

Another case of heartbreak.

Chapter Eleven

Natalie sat on the back porch with a cup of coffee for the second morning in a row. The big difference was she didn't have a hangover this time. She did have something that was much more disturbing.

Her thoughts.

More specifically, her thoughts about Giovanni. She enjoyed the hike with him yesterday. A lot. He was a good-looking, fun, and intelligent man. Maybe the emphasis should be put on his intelligence and kindhearted nature. He certainly was smart enough to notice that she and Jacks weren't connecting very much lately.

She scratched her hand and came to the realization that it wasn't the first time she had scratched it. She slowly raised it, hoping that it was nothing at all.

Fudge!

She didn't have to be a medical expert to know she had poison oak. She checked her other hand and her arms and couldn't find any irritated areas. Good thing she washed the area well just after it happened; it could have been a lot worse. But if she had it there was a good chance Giovanni had it too.

Her thoughts were interrupted by the sound of music. Beautiful music, actually. It was faint, but she could hear acoustic guitar and make out a few of the words, like 'love' and 'destiny' and 'my heart is singing.' It was coming from the other side of the fence. From Giovanni's studio, of course. He obviously was playing his stereo a little loud for so early in the morning.

Natalie felt like a cobra—and Giovanni the snake charmer.

With the music beckoning her, she stood up and walked to the back of the yard, through the gate, and to his studio. She slid the door open with the back of her hand and stepped inside. Precious got up from what appeared to be a makeshift bed made out of a bedroom pillow and made her way to Natalie, her tail shaking along the way. Natalie stroked Precious' silky ears and smiled.

Natalie blinked twice. The song wasn't coming from the stereo.

It was Giovanni!

Giovanni played his guitar and sang what was perhaps the most beautiful song she had heard in a long time. His voice contained so much passion as he belted out the lyrics about love and finding someone special. His fingers worked the strings in magical ways.

Nice hands.

She suddenly had a déjà vu. Something about Giovanni's hands. She looked a little closer and noticed he had a little

144

bit of redness on one of them.

Fudge! Poison oak!

She wasn't going to mention it if he didn't. It was her fault since she pushed him into it and Natalie felt slightly guilty.

Giovanni's song snapped her out of her thoughts and she was amazed how talented he was. He finished the song and she couldn't help but clap.

"Wow, bravo!" she said.

Giovanni turned around and smiled. "Sorry, I didn't hear you come in. Didn't smell you either."

"Ahh. No perfume this morning."

"My loss."

She smiled. "I was going to knock, sorry. It was beautiful."

He set the guitar on the stand against the wall, stood up, and scratched his hand. "Thank you."

She reached down and rubbed the dog's head again. "Who's the original artist of the song?"

Giovanni smiled again. "Giovanni Roma."

She blinked. "Really?"

"It still needs a little work."

"I have to disagree with you." She looked around the studio, not sure what she was looking for. Maybe just admiring things. Like the guitar with the reddish tones on the table.

She pointed to the guitar. "I love the color of that guitar. Is that just the finish or is it a special wood?"

"Both. The wood comes from the Appalachians. It's cut

from an Adirondack spruce. And I agree with you, it's one of my favorites."

She nodded. "You must have a lot of patience."

"Why do you say that?"

"Didn't you tell me it takes a month to make each one?"

"I guess you could say that. I only make ten guitars a year. There's a lot that goes into it."

He must have a day job or something. No way he could make a living off of selling ten guitars per year.

"Do you mind me asking what one of these guitars would cost?"

"Not at all—the information is public and on my website, so you could Google me and find out. The average price is eighteen thousand."

Natalie was well aware her mouth hung open but she couldn't control it. "Eighteen thousand?"

"Yes."

"For a guitar?"

"Yes."

"For *one* guitar."

"That's right."

"Hmm." She walked around the studio and inspected a few other pieces of wood on the table as she mentally calculated ten guitars multiplied by eighteen thousand dollars apiece.

I guess he doesn't need a day job.

She turned to Giovanni and said, "Why did you put that

flower in my hair on the hike?"

His eyes opened wide and he chuckled. "I think you need to work on your transitions a little. That change of subject was like a brick to the head."

"I'm just curious."

"I don't know."

"Don't know what?"

He fidgeted with a bowl of guitar picks and then made eye contact with her. "I knew purple was your favorite color and…I saw a purple flower. I just felt like giving it to you, that's all—just an impulse."

"How did you know purple was my favorite color?"

He laughed. "It's pretty obvious." He wiggled one of his ear lobes.

Natalie felt her ears and then remembered she was wearing her favorite purple earrings again, the same ones she wore at the park. She forced a smile. All the time she'd spent with Jacks—her own *fiancé*—and he didn't even know purple was her favorite color.

"Well," said Giovanni. "Sorry if it upset you—it won't happen again."

"You don't have to apologize for being sweet. It's just—I don't know. I guess it caught me off guard."

"Oh. Okay."

They locked eyes for a brief moment and both jumped when Federico entered and loudly announced, "What a beautiful day!"

Okay, maybe it only seemed like he screamed. She should be used to it by now. You'd think he was powered by non-stop espressos, but his energy was one-hundred percent natural.

Giovanni smiled. "I agree, Federico. A *very* beautiful day."

"I want to invite you for dinner this evening," said Federico. "I am going to prepare my very special eggplant parmesan dish. You will come, no?"

Giovanni licked his lips. "How can I pass that up?"

"Good! See you at six!"

"I'll be there."

||*|*|*|*

Giovanni spent the rest of the day working on the guitar for James. He was very proud of it and excited knowing it would go to someone so young and talented. He took a break in the middle of the day to take Precious out for another walk, then stopped by the store to pick up a bottle of wine to bring to dinner. At the market a woman dropped her purse and all of the contents scattered about the floor. Giovanni helped her pick everything up and she thanked him.

Another good deed!

At exactly six on the dot he went through the side gate into Federico's yard and slid open the sliding glass door. Federico was busy at the kitchen counter preparing a Caprese salad. Giovanni spotted the garlic bread and smiled.

"Smells great, Federico."

"Grazie." Federico turned to hug Giovanni and then got back to the salad.

Giovanni gestured to the bottle of wine in his hand. "I brought this for you."

Federico looked back and smiled. "Vino! You can find an opener in the first drawer. You remember where the glasses are, no?"

"Yes."

"Natalie is in the shower. She will be out soon and we'll eat."

Giovanni felt slightly guilty because of where his thoughts were headed. They were in the shower. With Natalie.

He couldn't be blamed, could he? Natalie was a beautiful, sexy woman and she was naked at that very moment. Any red-blooded man with a brain and a healthy libido would be thinking of her in that shower. Lathering up and rinsing off in slow motion. The steam hovering around her body. Absolutely normal thoughts, of course!

But Federico made no mention of the passionless fiancé. Was he on his way? It sure didn't sound like it, but he needed to know if he was going to be there.

"Will Jacks be joining us?"

Please say no.

Federico peeked down the hallway and shot his gaze back to Giovanni. "No," he whispered. "And between you and me, I'm perfectly fine with that."

"Me too," whispered Giovanni.

"It's mighty quiet over here," said Natalie. "What are you two up to?"

Giovanni eyed her purple summer dress. "We were talking about our favorite colors. Mine is purple. So is Federico's. That's why he made the eggplant. Right, Federico?"

"Absolutely, my friend!"

Natalie smacked Giovanni on the arm. "Behave."

Giovanni smiled. "I'll try. Nice to see you."

"You too." She reached up, hugged him, and smiled. He tried not to hold on too long, which wasn't easy considering how great she felt. And her smell?

Amazing as usual.

Giovanni opened the bottle of wine and pulled out three glasses from the cupboard. The thought of an evening with just Natalie and Federico sounded perfect to him. And with Federico in the room he would be able to control himself and quit staring so much at Natalie. Because damn, she looked so beautiful this evening. Was she getting more beautiful every day?

Giovanni poured the wine and sat.

Federico brought the food to the table, raised his wine glass, and smiled. "To two of my favorite people. Salute!"

"Salute!" said Giovanni and Natalie at the same time.

As Federico passed the food around the table, Giovanni felt a sinking feeling coming on. More like embarrassment. Here Federico was saying he was one of his favorite people and Giovanni didn't invite him to his wedding. He felt like a world-class jerk. He'd been meaning to say something over the last week but couldn't bring himself to do it. He took a sip of wine and tried to clear his thoughts. Hopefully nobody noticed his mood change.

Federico spooned some Caprese on his plate and looked up at Giovanni. "Is everything okay?"

So much for nobody noticing. He needed to tell him the truth. Federico was a good guy and he deserved to know what happened.

Giovanni forced a smile. "No. Not really."

Federico frowned. "What is on your mind?"

"I owe you an explanation, Federico. I didn't invite you to my wedding and you need to know why."

"I knew you had a good reason and I can respect that."

The response didn't surprise Giovanni. Federico was just a kind, warm-hearted human being.

"Still," said Giovanni. "I need to tell you. Patricia told me she didn't want strangers at her wedding and since she had officially never met you, you qualified as a stranger. That wasn't the real reason, though. She reduced the size of the guest list, then immediately increased the budget. She wanted a more lavish wedding and spent two hundred dollars a plate on the food and over fifteen thousand on flowers. I didn't like the idea and told her, but the tension was unbearable and I gave in. We scratched forty-five people from the list. Almost all from my side."

"But there wasn't a wedding so it doesn't matter."

"It *does* matter. My actions were wrong. I'm sorry. I was a jackass."

Natalie waved off what Giovanni said. "That's nothing. Jacks changed our honeymoon from a month in Europe to ten days in Death Valley. He said it would be healthy for us to go camping and connect with nature and eat granola bars. Then he canceled his bachelor party in Vegas. All because he wanted to buy a Harley." She took a sip of her wine and rolled it around in her mouth before swallowing it. "I found the brochure under some books on his desk. Oh, and to top it off he eliminated a hundred people from our guest list."

"After hearing your story I don't feel so bad," said Giovanni, laughing.

And with that he received another smack on the arm. This woman liked to hit! He enjoyed this playful side of Natalie.

Man, oh man.

His thoughts went from hits to spankings in a flash. He really had to stop doing that. She was going to catch him and then how would he respond? He felt comfortable around Natalie. She was just like Federico, a good person you could trust.

Natalie pointed to Giovanni's face. "Where did your mind just go?"

Son of a bison! The woman was as sharp as a Ginsu knife.

He scratched his cheek and lied. "I don't remember."

She continued to stare at him.

He shrugged. "Spankings."

She blushed and took a sip of her wine.

Federico burst out with laughter. "Pass the garlic bread, please."

They enjoyed a wonderful meal prepared by Federico. Giovanni could really see what a fun person Natalie was.

Giovanni stared at Natalie as she scratched her hand.

She had poison oak too. He opened his mouth and then closed it. Probably would be best if he didn't mention it.

"What?" asked Natalie, obviously noticing him about to speak.

"Nothing."

Quick. Think of something to distract!

"How long you been a cop?" he asked.

She looked at him suspiciously. "Ten years."

"It must be very rewarding."

"Definitely. I have the opportunity to help people and guide them to make better choices. I believe people can change if treated with respect and kindness."

Giovanni nodded. "I like that."

"I'm very proud of my bambina," said Federico.

It was great to see how close Federico and Natalie were. Giovanni had never felt close to his mom. He'd been very successful and totally fulfilled with his guitar business, but it never seemed like it was good enough for his mother. He was much closer to his dad. Alfonso always loved and respected what Giovanni did for a living, but never expressed it out loud for fear of the wrath of his Eleonora. Giovanni always felt bad for his dad because he just followed his mom around like a puppy dog. He didn't seem happy and that was no way to live. He longed to ask his father how he survived being married to his mother all these years. He needed to understand why he stayed.

"Have you ever had to use your gun?" asked Giovanni

He hoped that wasn't a stupid question, but he found it fascinating and scary that she carried a weapon that could take away someone's life in a split second.

"No. Never had to use it."

"That's good. Taser?"

She shook her head.

"Ever kicked a guy in the balls?"

"No, but if it makes you feel better I can make that happen for the first time tonight."

"Tempting, but I'll pass."

"I had a feeling you'd say that." She studied Giovanni for a moment. "What about you? How did you get into building guitars?"

Giovanni smiled. "My parents took me to Spain when I was six. Kind of crazy when you think of it because kids that age can't really appreciate the beauty and history of a place like that, you know?"

Natalie nodded. "But you were able to appreciate it?"

"Yes and no. My dad was obsessed with flamenco and wanted to share it with me. The dancing, the singing, the guitar playing, the handclapping—everything. For me, I couldn't care less about most of it at that age, except for the guitar. There was something special about the instrument and I was hooked. So we were walking on some tiny cobblestoned street in the south of Spain, in Málaga to be exact, and we stumbled upon a man making a flamenco guitar by hand in a shop window. We ended up watching the guy work on a guitar most of the day and my dad got his business card. Six months later on my birthday my dad gave me a guitar. One that the old man made."

"Amazing. But how did you go from guitar playing to guitar *making?*"

"Fast forward twelve years to the summer after I graduated from high school. I had planned on spending a couple of months traveling around Europe—a graduation present from my parents. Italy, France, and back to Spain, before starting college. Just for kicks I went to go see if that guy was still making guitars. He was and he actually remembered me!"

"How in the world did he remember you?"

"No idea. But it's what happened afterward that was even crazier. I decided to stay in Spain a year as the man's apprentice. I learned everything I could from him and didn't get paid a single penny. He offered me food and a room and I took it. And I loved it! After that I came back and worked part-time at the local music shop until I could get the business up and running. And the rest is history."

"What a story."

Federico pointed to Giovanni. "And this kind man donates a guitar every single year to a special program for children. What is the name of it?"

"Music Prodigies of America. It's a nonprofit that supplies musical instruments to underprivileged youths who possess extraordinary music skills."

Natalie stared at Giovanni for a moment. "That's wonderful. Do you ever get to meet the kids?"

"Usually not. But tomorrow will be the first time I actually meet one of them in person because he lives in the state. In Sacramento."

"Really? You must be excited."

"I am. But to be honest with you I'm a little nervous too."

"How come?"

"It's a special case. He's an orphan."

"Oh…"

Natalie looked like she wanted to say something else but didn't.

Federico patted her on top of the hand.

Natalie stood up. "I'll get the dessert."

Federico stood up as well and tapped Giovanni on the shoulder. "While she gets that ready I'd like to show you something, my friend."

He followed Federico to the wall of pictures—almost all of them were of Federico and Olive. There wasn't a day that went by where he wasn't saying something sweet about

Olive. He'd seen the pictures before, but there were some new ones added.

Federico pointed to the picture of the two of them on top of a glacier kissing. "This was our cruise to Alaska. We took a helicopter ride and landed on top of this glacier. Then of course Olive kissed me there. She was always kissing me."

"I like that," said Giovanni. He turned his head in the direction of Natalie so she could hear him loud and clear. "Kissing is good!"

"Yes!" agreed Federico.

"In fact, a woman kissed me just the other night."

Federico lost the smile on his face. "What do you mean?"

Natalie cleared her throat and walked to the kitchen table with a cheesecake. "Okay, time for dessert."

The men joined Natalie at the table and she cut them each a slice.

Federico took the first bite and moaned. "Very, very good." He still had a serious look on his face and turned to Giovanni. "Who was that woman who kissed you?"

Giovanni glanced at Natalie who shook her head as a warning.

"Some drunk. She couldn't keep her hands off of me."

Giovanni should have known better than to play with Natalie. She was a cop and didn't take shit! The kick he received under the table was swift and right on the money.

She was good. *Really* good.

It felt like someone jabbed him with an ice pick. He

couldn't contain the scream. He clutched his shin and rubbed it up and down in a quick motion. The rubbing was supposed to make it feel better, but the pain was increasing with every second that passed.

Federico jumped in his seat and looked under the table. "What is it? Are you okay?"

"I think so," he said, continuing to rub his leg. "It was just a cramp."

He looked over to Natalie who was avoiding eye contact and eating. Not sure how she could fit that fork of cheesecake in her mouth. That giant smirk had to be getting in the way.

She thinks this is funny?

He had to admit he probably would be laughing too if it weren't for the pain.

"Are you going to be okay?" asked Federico.

"Yeah,…yeah, I think so. The pain is starting to go away."

"Good. This is very fascinating."

"My pain is fascinating?"

Federico chuckled. "No, no. I want to know more about the woman who kissed you. You had me worried for a moment, but it sounds like the kiss was nothing."

Worried? Why would he be worried? Was Federico trying to set me up with Natalie?

"But please tell me how it happened," said Federico.

Natalie paused her fork of cheesecake in midair, waiting for Giovanni's response. She pursed her lips together and mouthed the word *no* to him. He was pretty sure he saw her nostrils flare. It was his move. How should he play it?

He knew he should've just stopped right there but he couldn't help himself.

Giovanni tucked his legs as far as possible under his chair. "I'm not sure how it happened, but it tickled."

No kick, but he wasn't expecting one since there was nothing incriminating there. He glanced at Natalie again who still had the cheesecake stranded in no-man's land between the plate and her mouth. She obviously had her finger on the trigger. The trigger being her foot and the target being his leg again. As painful as it was, he was enjoying her company. He knew he would probably get it good from her but he couldn't help it. He knew he was just seconds away from another painful kick.

"Really?" said Federico. "It tickled? All my years of kissing Olive and I do not recall a single time when it tickled."

Giovanni nodded. "Well, honestly, it was most likely from her mustache. I'm pretty sure she was a transvestite."

Sharp-shooter Natalie gritted her teeth and let her foot fly under the table, connecting directly with Giovanni's shin in the exact same spot.

"Son of a biscuit!" Giovanni yelled, grabbing his shin again. How did she do that? He had to remember to pick her for his team if they ever joined a co-ed soccer league. Still, in between the jabs of throbbing pain he tried hard to contain the laughter that was building up inside.

Federico glanced under the table again. "Another cramp?"

"Yes," he answered, his voice a few octaves higher this time.

Federico pointed to his cheesecake. "You haven't touched your dessert yet."

"Good call." He took a bite and chewed slowly. "Mmm." He took another bite and moaned again, looking at Natalie. "So tasty."

Natalie looked away. "Thank you."

Was she blushing? He was pretty sure of it.

Giovanni enjoyed the cheesecake and the conversation. The entire evening was wonderful. He was sure he'd have a bruise or two on his leg tomorrow, but he was okay with that. Natalie was a gem. An angel with a devil's smile.

As they wrapped up the evening Federico smiled and put one hand on Giovanni's shoulder and the other on Natalie's. "This feels like family to me."

Giovanni glanced at Natalie and said, "Yeah. Feels good."

Natalie flashed an insincere smile and turned her back. She stood by the sliding-glass door looking out at the backyard. What was that all about? Was she embarrassed?

Giovanni hugged Federico. "Thanks again for everything. It was an enjoyable evening."

"Yes! We'll do it again soon! And next time bring the dog! I don't mind."

"Sounds like a plan. I'm sure Precious would like that very much." He turned and approached Natalie. "It was really *a kick* seeing you, Natalie."

Natalie snorted and smiled.

That smile could melt glaciers.

Giovanni smiled and hugged her. "Sleep well."

She squeezed his arm. "Thanks. You too."

What the hell was that arm squeeze all about? Was that some secret code? Maybe he was reading into it too much. But it seemed like something. Her gaze dropped to his mouth.

Son of a biscuit! She's checking out my lips, I'm sure of it! I can't kiss her…she's engaged! That is not kosher. Not gonna do it. Get those thoughts out of your head. Walk away!

His heart pounded as he scooted to the side and slid open the door. "Thanks again."

"Oh…" she said.

Giovanni whipped around and almost knocked her over. "Yes?"

"I'd be happy to go with you tomorrow…to deliver the guitar. I have the day off."

"You would?"

She nodded. "I mean—if you want company. I have some experience working with orphans."

Giovanni smiled. "That would be great. Thank you. I need to leave the house by nine in the morning if that's okay."

Then she did the unexpected. She got on her tiptoes and kissed Giovanni on the cheek. "See you tomorrow at nine then."

Okay, what the hell was that? Was that a friendly kiss? A promise-of-more-to-come kiss? A sorry-I-mangled-your-shins kiss?

He had to admit he sucked at reading women. He didn't look back and marched to the back gate, his heart still drumming a song he hadn't heard in a long time.

He felt something.

Something good. Something wonderful. Something strong.

And he was pretty sure that something was going to keep him up most of the night.

Chapter Twelve

Sacramento was a little over two hours from Los Gatos. Not the most exciting drive in the world, but much more tolerable with the presence of an attractive woman in the car. Giovanni pretended to look down at the compartment between the seats, then took a quick peek at Natalie.

Scratch that. Not attractive. More like pretty.

Pretty *freaking hot!*

He glanced over at her again. The more he looked the more beautiful she got. He couldn't stop looking. At least she didn't notice—that would be embarrassing.

"You don't think I can see you doing that?" she asked.

Crap.

What was he thinking? Of course she would notice! She was a cop and she was trained to spot peculiar behavior. Or in his case, *idiotic* behavior.

"I'm not sure what you mean," he lied.

"Why were you looking at me?"

Good luck getting out of this one. Maybe he should just tell the truth.

"If there's a law against looking at a beautiful woman you'll have to arrest me."

She snorted. "Nice try..."

He glanced over at her and she was grinning. Good sign.

She didn't speak for a moment and then said, "You think you're smooth, don't you?"

"Like a smoothie."

"You know how ridiculous that sounded?"

Yes. It was pathetic. "That's all I could come up with at the moment."

Natalie laughed. "Well, at least you're honest. Tell me about James."

"Okay." He thought about it for a moment. "I don't know much about him, really. I saw a picture. Cute kid. Brilliant guitar player at the age of eight. Lives with foster parents."

"Do you know what happened to the parents?"

"No," said Giovanni. "Poor kid. That's why I was nervous about meeting him. I'd hate to say the wrong thing, you know?"

"Just be yourself. That's the best thing you can do. Don't treat him any differently than you would any other kids you meet for the first time."

"Really?"

"Absolutely. He'll be able to spot insincerity or pity a mile away."

"Good to know. Thanks."

"You're welcome."

Giovanni was glad Natalie offered to come along. Very sweet. He felt a lot less nervous about meeting James too.

"How do you know so much about foster kids?" he asked.

Natalie didn't answer.

Giovanni glanced at her. She was looking out the window at the rolling hills along Highway 680. Deep in thought. It looked like the question hit a little too close to home. He remembered her reaction at dinner too. Obviously she didn't want to talk about it. Time to change the subject.

He pointed to the stereo. "Feel free to take command of the radio and listen to whatever you want."

"You're very sweet."

"Hey, I'm not *giving* you the radio. You get to temporarily use it until I get tired of whatever music you choose. Which may be pretty quick."

She laughed. "I was talking about you changing the subject. You don't like people to feel uncomfortable—that's very sweet. And sorry for not answering you earlier."

"It's okay."

"I was a foster kid."

"Oh…"

"My parents died in a car accident when I was very young. I was with them actually but the car seat saved me. I don't remember them, so that's probably why I don't have a lot of baggage that goes with it. My foster parents were amazing, wonderful people and they even reunited me with my grandfather. For that I will be eternally grateful."

"Federico is one cool dude. Where did they find him?"

"He was in Italy. But the most amazing part is he and

165

Grandma left everything…their home, their business, and their life just to come to here to be with me."

"That *is* amazing."

"So I was just thinking about James and what he must be going through. Not everyone can be as lucky as me and it can be very difficult for some children. Even traumatic."

"Yeah." Giovanni smiled. "Glad you turned out okay."

"Thank you."

"Except for maybe that obsession you have with inflicting pain upon the shins of innocent people at the dinner table. You may have some issues there."

Natalie poked Giovanni in the side of the arm. "You called me a drunk transvestite!"

Giovanni couldn't help but laugh.

"I would kick you right now, but you're driving and I don't want us to crash."

"So this would be the perfect time to tease you a little more then?"

"Yes, but just wait till you stop the car. You're going to get it."

He smiled. "I certainly hope so." He looked over at Natalie and she was blushing. She was also smiling. "And yes, I'm looking at you again. I love your smile."

"Thank you."

"And I like you."

"Thanks again."

"A lot."

She turned and looked out the window at the rolling hills again. There was no way she liked the scenery that much. Did he take it too far? Probably so. He was flirting with an engaged woman and that was wrong.

Wrong. Wrong. Wrong.

But he couldn't help it. He felt a connection with Natalie and deep down he wished she were single. It wasn't fair she was getting married. Especially to a guy who didn't even appreciate her. He looked over at Natalie again and her smile was gone. He'd bet a million dollars she was reading his mind. She was a woman. The chances were damn good.

"Not going to happen," she said.

"What?" he answered, even though he was almost certain he knew what she was talking about.

"You and me. You need to quit flirting with me. I'm engaged, or did you forget that tiny little fact?"

He should have bet the million.

"Sorry," he answered. "I don't do it on purpose. You bring it out of me. Naturally."

They didn't speak much the rest of the drive. Giovanni felt like an idiot, but he figured it was best to leave it alone and not say anything else. He apologized and that was all he could do for now. Two hours later he parked in front of a modest home in Elk Grove, a suburb of Sacramento.

"Remember," said Natalie. "Just be yourself. You'll do fine."

"I'll do my best. Thanks."

The front door swung open and James waved. Cute kid. Just like in the photo. He had short, curly brown hair, pale skin, and black-rimmed glasses. They seemed to clash with his Sacramento Kings basketball jersey.

"Hi," said James.

"Hello. You must be James."

"Yeah."

"I'm Giovanni." He pointed to the right with his thumb. "And this is Natalie."

"Nice to meet you," said Natalie.

"Nice to meet you too." James stared at Giovanni. "Giovanni's has my favorite pizza. Hawaiian. I like extra pineapple. Are you the owner?"

"No."

"I got in trouble yesterday for letting a fly in the house."

"You want us to come in so you can shut the door?"

"Okay. We knew it was you when the doorbell rang and not somebody trying to rob us." He pointed above the door. "We have security cameras. You want to see the monitors where we were spying on you?"

Giovanni laughed. He liked the kid already. "Sure. Sounds cool."

"Okay."

They stepped inside the house and Giovanni closed the door behind them.

James pointed to the guitar case Giovanni was carrying. "Cool case. It's smaller than mine."

"The guitar is smaller too—made for a kid." Giovanni looked down the hallway and then back to James. "You know any kids around here who play guitar?"

James laughed. "You're funny. I was told not to get too excited about the guitar you brought me. So I need to pretend because kids get excited about things and I'm a kid." He started to turn and then stopped. "And it's very important that I say thank you for the guitar many times before you leave."

"Okay!" said a man approaching the entry. He extended his hand. A woman appeared by his side. "I'm Roger McLeod and this is my wife Betty. You must be Giovanni and Natalie."

Giovanni introduced himself and Natalie, and they followed the McLeods into the living room and sat on the loveseat. It was a tight squeeze so Giovanni's hip was right against Natalie's. He wasn't going to complain about that at all. It felt good.

James sat on the floor facing Giovanni and his guitar case.

Roger gestured to the cookies and scones on the coffee table. "Please help yourself. Betty is going to make some tea."

Natalie and Giovanni both reached for the same chocolate chip cookie and bumped hands.

"Go ahead," she said, blushing and pointing to the cookie.

"No," said Giovanni, pointing to the cookie. "Please. Beauty before Beast."

She laughed and took the cookie.

Betty eyed the ring on Natalie's finger. "When is the wedding?"

Natalie and Giovanni looked at each other.

"Oh…no!" said Natalie, breaking the silence.

Betty checked out Giovanni for a moment. Then she studied Natalie. She furrowed her eyebrows and looked like she was having a difficult time grasping the situation.

Giovanni forced a smile and decided to help her out. "Natalie's engaged but not to me."

That was awkward, but at least Betty didn't dig any further.

The McLeods must have been in their late fifties. How were they able to keep up with an eight-year-old boy? They must have had a lot of energy.

"We want to thank you for coming all this way and for your generosity," said Roger.

Giovanni smiled. "It's a pleasure. When I read about James' talent and his love of the guitar I was impressed. And fascinated. I'm glad I can help."

Roger nodded. "He has a special concert Saturday night with the music conservatory, so your gift was perfect timing. The other guitar wouldn't have been…let's just say, photogenic." He pointed to the guitar on the stand in the corner. It was the one in the photo in the article. Although now it had a small strip of duct tape on the body.

The guitar was in very bad shape and Giovanni was grateful that he could help. And judging by the look on

James' face, the boy was grateful too.

James was like a hawk scoping out his prey—his eyes didn't budge from the guitar case.

"He will be the youngest person ever in their history to perform on that stage," continued Roger.

Natalie smiled. "Who knows…soon he could be performing all over the world. Would you like that, James?"

James nodded, his eyes still on the guitar case. "I wanna go to Italy and Spain and France and Germany and Switzerland."

"Sounds amazing." Giovanni pointed to the case. "Can I give you the guitar now?"

James jumped up from his spot on the floor and plopped down directly in front of Giovanni. "Yes, please. Thank you."

Giovanni was going to open the case, but changed his mind and decided to let James do it. Just like Christmas, he always enjoyed when people opened up their presents in front of him. More than opening up his own.

He slid the case out from the side of his chair and pushed it to James. "Go for it."

James pulled the case closer and turned it so it was face up. He undid each of the latches carefully—like he was trying to defuse a bomb.

Then he slowly opened it.

Giovanni wished he took a picture to capture the expression on the boy's face. His eyes couldn't have been any wider.

James smiled. "You made this with your hands?"

Giovanni nodded. "I did need the help of a few tools, but yes. Handmade."

"Cool."

James pulled out the guitar, sat on the ottoman, and immediately played. No warm up. No checking to see if it was in tune. No. None of that nonsense. He just played.

Like a pro.

Giovanni considered himself a pretty good player, but James was better. *Much* better.

And he was eight years old.

Giovanni turned to Natalie. Her mouth was hanging open too. Not a surprise.

When James finished the song everyone clapped.

Natalie put her hand to her chest. "That was amazing!"

James ran his hands along the curves of the guitar's body. Could a boy that young really appreciate the uniqueness and beauty of a handmade guitar? It certainly seemed so.

"Thank you," said James. He smiled at Giovanni. His eyes sparkled and expressed his deep gratitude. "This guitar is the perfect size for me. But only for five more years. Then I'm going to turn into a teenager."

Giovanni laughed. "That's true."

"Thank you very much."

"You're welcome."

He was one of the coolest kids Giovanni had met in a long

time. Giovanni felt his chest tighten and a warmth spread through his body. How lucky he was to be able to give this boy a gift that he made with his own hands. To see the appreciation on the kid's face was worth it.

He smiled at the beautiful boy. "My pleasure. It was a pleasure to hear you play too."

Roger cleared his throat. "James, don't forget to say thank you."

"Thank you, Giovanni. Thank you, Natalie."

Natalie jumped, obviously not expecting to be thanked. James hugged them both.

"I didn't do anything at all," said Natalie. "This all happened because of Giovanni."

"You came to visit me."

"Oh." She smiled and blushed. "That's true! Then you're welcome."

*****

Natalie fiddled with the radio on the way home. She felt nervous for some reason. She peeked over at Giovanni. He had a very satisfied grin on his face. He was a good man. Generous. Handsome.

There should be a law against a man being that good-looking.

Of course then she'd have to arrest him. And that would involve handcuffs. And touching.

Get your mind out of the gutter!

Giovanni laughed.

Natalie folded her arms. "What?"

"You don't think I can see you checking me out?"

She huffed. "I was *not* checking you out."

"If you say so. At least I was honest about it when you caught me."

"Okay, maybe I was admiring you. But I'm still getting married to Jacks."

"Of course you are."

"I am. So let's change subjects."

"Fine."

"Fine." She fidgeted with the radio a little more before opening her mouth again. "James is amazing."

"I agree." Giovanni glanced over at her again. "Would you take James in if you had the chance?"

"In a heartbeat."

"Me too. What would your *fiancé* say about that?"

That was a good question. And she was pretty sure she didn't want to know the answer. They had discussed children two times, and on both occasions Jacks mentioned he wouldn't be ready for a while—that he needed to move up in his career before committing to such a thing.

Such a thing.

When Jacks had said that it really rubbed Natalie the wrong way. What did the job have to do with it? He wasn't the one who was going to be pregnant. The one who was going to give birth. The one who was going to breastfeed. The one who would most likely change the diapers.

Giovanni reached across and snapped his fingers in front of Natalie's face. "You going to answer the question?"

"I don't know what Jacks would say. Really."

"Then it's settled. You and I will have children together."

Natalie reached for the radio again. "I'm just going to turn up the volume a little more to drown you out."

Giovanni laughed. "No need. I'll stop talking."

"That's a good idea."

Not that she didn't like to hear Giovanni speak. He had a sexy voice. Natalie was sure there was something special about him too. In fact, the more she got to know him the more he surprised her. She didn't dare compare him to her fiancé anymore.

No.

Comparing the two would bring trouble.

Chapter Thirteen

Giovanni set his morning coffee on the kitchen counter and paced back and forth through the living room. He had a lot on his mind, but at least he wasn't alone—Precious was on his heels. Every time he stopped, Precious would stop. When he resumed, the dog would resume.

Giovanni laughed. "You're a silly dog, aren't you?"

"Arf!"

"Of course you are."

He reached down and scratched her on the head and continued his pacing. "*Very* silly. And cute too."

"Arf!"

They continued their pacing in the family room and he did a loop around the island in the kitchen. Yeah, a lot on his mind.

Natalie was right. It would be good to call Patricia and find out why she didn't want to get married to him. Closure was good. He already had closure with her personal items. Hopefully Patricia's lover with the Ferrari was keeping her happy and she wasn't too mad about what Giovanni did with her belongings. He pulled the phone out of his jean pocket and called her.

"What do you want, Giovanni?"

Still pissed off.

"Hi Patricia."

"Make this quick—I have a bikini wax and wine tasting this afternoon."

"At the same time?"

"No, not at the same time! Speak or I'm hanging up."

"Okay. I'm calling to just find out…what happened. Between you and me."

"Oh God. Is this so you can have closure and all that bullshit?"

How did she know? "Yes."

Patricia let out a deep breath. "I should just make you suffer and wonder for the rest of your life after what you did to my things. Okay, let's get this over with. Number one, I just couldn't handle your mom."

"My mom? What? Pressure of having grandchildren?"

"Hell yes. She came to my work—said she wanted to take me out to lunch, which I thought was odd. And while I was eating with her she asked me a million questions. Things about my stress level, my average body temperature, my sleeping patterns, history of boys in the family. She even asked if I could start charting my menstrual cycle. When I said no she insisted on driving me to my next gyno appointment. I said no and walked out on her again."

"Wow."

"But enough about your psychotic mother. Really, if you

think about it, we're two *very* different people. You and I want different things. I want things that glitter and sparkle and you want things that...don't. Me? Four Seasons. You? Holiday Inn. You're happy with simple and I'm happy with sophistication. Nothing wrong with that, just not too compatible."

"Then why did you accept my proposal?"

She sighed. "I thought I could change you and make you realize how important it is to have the finest things in life."

"Well, if that's what you want, I'm sure there's someone out there who will give it to you."

"It's not something I want. I *need* them. That is who I am and I don't want you to judge me. And yes, I found someone."

"That was fast. Does he drive a Ferrari?"

"Not anymore. I drive it. But that's because he understands me. This was meant to be."

He couldn't argue with her on that point. This breakup was a hundred times less painful than the first one. In fact, he wondered if he suffered at all. Sure, his initial reaction when he wanted to burn all of her belongings was strong, but that didn't last long at all. And since he met Natalie, he hadn't even thought of Patricia except when they talked about her.

He wondered what Natalie was doing right now. He wouldn't mind being kicked in the shins a few more times, just to be with her. Just to get another glimpse of that beautiful smile and her sexy—.

"Giovanni?"

Oops.

He forgot he was still on the phone with Patricia. "Yeah, sorry. We must have a bad connection."

They said their goodbyes and Giovanni wished her well.

He had closure. And it was good to know that what happened wasn't his fault.

They say things happen for a reason and Giovanni had to wonder if the reason he got the shaft from Patricia was so he could meet Natalie. It was only because he didn't get married that he met her on the street when she was about to give him a ticket. Sure there was a good chance he would have met Natalie at Federico's house some other time, but maybe she would have been married by then too.

She was still engaged to be married to Jacks though…

*****

It was a new day and Natalie's thoughts were on James. What a wonderful boy. She was glad she'd had the opportunity to go with Giovanni.

She let out a deep breath. "Giovanni," she mumbled.

Her mind drifted to him in his red underwear again.

Behave.

She needed to get her mind off of the guitar-making hunk next door.

Now!

A trip to the gym with her best friend Rebecca would hopefully do the trick. Natalie was having doubts and maybe Rebecca could help her sort through things before she headed off to work.

She stepped onto the elliptical machine and pressed the start button. "You hate Jacks, don't you?"

Okay, that wasn't so smooth. Rebecca practically fell off the machine when she was hit with the question. Maybe Natalie should have eased into the conversation or maybe rephrased that.

Rebecca tied her blonde hair behind her head, increased the speed of her machine, and looked over to Natalie. "What are you talking about?"

"Do you think Jacks is the right one for me? Yes or no?"

"Oh my God. You're getting cold feet?"

Maybe. Probably. Yes. "No!"

She wasn't sure why she answered so loudly. Or why she lied. A few heads turned in their direction. Sure, she had doubts, but it would be good to see if Rebecca had them too.

In a lower voice Natalie continued, "Just tell me your thoughts. You never mention him or talk about us as a couple, and I find that very odd and maybe a sign that you don't approve."

Rebecca shrugged. "How can I even judge him? He's never around—I barely know the guy. I've seen him three times, and you always said he was great so I had to believe you."

"Yeah. I think I've seen him once in the last week and a half. He's moving toward his goal of being district attorney and says he's doing it for us—for our future. But I secretly wish he had some lame job, barely making any money at all, just so I could see him more often. And if he's not working, he's cleaning his car. I'm not having fun. Our honeymoon period is over and we haven't even gotten married yet!"

"Most men get their identity from their job, but what is it with Jacks and his Camaro? I think if it were possible he would sleep with it."

Natalie snorted.

"Other than that, he seems like a decent guy," said Rebecca.

"That's a big endorsement. Saying a guy is 'decent' is like saying a meal was just okay. That's not a very good answer." She needed to know more. She pressed the stop button on her machine and turned to Rebecca. "Decent. That's all?"

"He's successful. He's loyal. And he's certainly in a hurry to make you his trophy wife. Many people see that as a positive."

"What the heck are you talking about?"

"Nothing at all." Rebecca played with the buttons on her elliptical machine. "You want to do an hour today and then do some stretching?"

"I am *not* going to be his trophy wife." She reached over and pressed the stop button on Rebecca's machine. "Trophy wife? Come on!"

"You're smart and you're beautiful. He's going to show you off wherever you go. That's why he bought you that boulder on your finger. Nothing wrong with that, if that's what bakes your cake."

"You know I'm not like that."

"Just some macho dog marking his territory, that's all. Mine, mine, mine!" She waved her arms in the air like a lunatic.

"I can't believe I'm hearing this!"

Rebecca laughed. "I'm kidding! Boy, you really do have cold feet, don't you?"

Natalie nodded.

"Alright then, let me ask you this: does he care about what makes you happy?"

Natalie let out a breath so powerful her lips vibrated. She sounded like a horse. "You sound like Giovanni! Oh God, that must be a sign."

"What exactly did Giovanni say?"

"That Jacks should be doing everything in his power to make me happy. Every single day."

Rebecca nodded. "I like Giovanni—he's smart, fun, and he's hot. Maybe you should marry *him*."

It's not like Natalie hadn't thought about that, but still…

Fudge.

Now she was thinking of Giovanni in his underwear again. She massaged her temples and tried to regain her focus. "You're saying this now?"

"I was kidding! Again!"

"I don't think you are. You're withholding evidence."

"Okay, now you're starting to sound like Jacks. I've changed my mind—maybe you *should* marry him."

Natalie jumped off of the machine. "I've lost my motivation for working out. Let's go. Change of plans." She grabbed her water bottle and towel and stepped off of the machine. She was having some serious doubts and needed the comfort of a giant cinnamon roll from the donut place next door.

Rebecca grabbed her stuff. "Donuts?"

She knew her so well.

Natalie nodded and pointed to the door. "Now."

Kind of cruel—opening a donut shop next to the gym. But she wasn't going to complain at the moment—it's just what she needed. A minute later they were seated with their coffees and a bag of buttery, sugary, deep-fried goodness.

Rebecca pointed to Natalie's hand. "Dry skin?"

Natalie shook her head. "Poison oak. Thankfully it's just a mild case."

"Still. Don't touch me."

"You're so sweet."

Rebecca stared at Natalie for a moment. "You don't seem like your normal, happy self lately. Tell me what's really going on."

"I'm having serious doubts."

"That's obvious."

Jacks was a decent man and he loved her. Still, another question was floating around in the back of Natalie's mind. How much did she really love him? Enough to spend the rest of her life with him? Or did she just love the idea of being married? Just the thought of the latter made her shiver. Not a reason to get married at all.

Rebecca dunked a piece of her donut in the coffee. Before she put it in her mouth she said, "What specifically has been on your mind?"

"The man next door."

"No."

She nodded.

"Did you sleep with him?"

"No! What kind of question is that?"

"Sorry! Have you thought about sleeping with him?"

Natalie didn't answer. She took a bite of her cinnamon roll and avoided eye contact with Rebecca. She knew the ploy wouldn't work, but at least it would buy her some time and a few more bites before she had to tell the truth.

Rebecca slapped the table. "I'll take that as a yes."

"No, don't take it as a yes. I've only technically been thinking about his kisses. While he's in his underwear."

"Oh. That's *much* different."

"Am I crazy?"

"No, you're not crazy. Remember? I had cold feet before I got married. And everything worked out fine, didn't it?"

Natalie smiled. "Yes. Scott is amazing."

"And everything will work out fine for you."

It sounded nice. But Natalie still had her doubts.

*****

Natalie arrived home, showered, and changed into her uniform. She had about an hour before she had to start her shift today. She'd heard the phone ring while she was in the shower so she checked her messages.

"Hi Natalie, it's me, Miguel."

Miguel was the musician she hired to play the piano for the ceremony.

Oh God. Please don't say there is a problem. Please don't say it.

"There's a problem."

Shit!

"I broke my wrist playing basketball yesterday. My right hand is in a cast, so obviously it's not possible for me to play at your wedding. I'm so sorry."

What a way to start the day! He better have a replacement! Somebody. Anybody! Don't leave me hanging, Miguel!

"I wish I knew someone who could play in my place, but as you know the summer is a popular time for weddings and all of my friends are booked on your date."

Unbelievable.

She sat on the bed and waited for him to finish speaking

before she would probably start to cry.

"Of course I'll issue a credit back to your credit card for the full amount. Again, I'm very sorry."

There was a knock at her door.

She deleted the message and sat there dejected. What was she going to do now?

Hopefully the person behind the door had the answer.

"Come in."

"Pancakes?" asked Federico.

"I have a problem."

"Oh." He moved to the bed and sat next to her. "Tell me how your Nono can help."

"That's just it, I'm not sure if anyone can. The musician for the ceremony just canceled on me. He broke his wrist. But this is one of the most popular weekends of the year for weddings. Nobody else will be available."

Federico smiled. "Come with me."

"Nono. I know you are going to say that pancakes are the answer, but honestly, I lost my appetite."

He smiled and grabbed her by the hand and led her to the family room where the sliding glass door was open. The backyard looked so peaceful and she watched as a hummingbird drank from the feeder.

"Beautiful," she said. "I love the hummingbirds."

"Me too. But if you focus, I mean *really* focus, you'll be able to enjoy something even *more* beautiful than the hummingbirds."

"Really?" She scanned the backyard looking for something else. What could it be? There was a squirrel on the telephone wire. Nah. Couldn't be that. She looked around a little more and shrugged. "I give up. What is it?"

"Not so fast. Close your eyes."

"What? Nono, have you been drinking this morning?"

He laughed. "Just do it."

She let out a deep breath and closed her eyes. It only took a few seconds before it hit her. She wasn't sure why she didn't notice it before. Beautiful music.

Coming from the house next door.

She smiled and then opened her eyes. "Yes, I've heard his music before. He's amazing. Just yesterday morning he was playing that same—"

Her mouth dropped open and she turned to Federico, who was smiling. "Oh. That's why you dragged me here."

"If anyone can help you, he can. He knows a lot of people in the music business."

She kissed him on the cheek. "Thanks, Nono. I owe you. Big time!"

She ran to the end of the backyard, through the gate, and slid open Giovanni's studio door. There he was in his usual spot playing.

He finished. "Hi."

She waved even though he was standing three feet from her. "Hi."

Giovanni eyed her from head to toe. "You going to arrest

me, Officer? Or maybe just kick me a few times?"

She couldn't hold back the laugh. "Okay, don't make me laugh—I need to stay focused. I have a serious problem."

Giovanni lost his smile. "How can I help?"

"The pianist I hired for the wedding broke his wrist."

"Ouch."

"I feel bad for him. But I feel worse for me because he doesn't have a replacement and the wedding is this Saturday. So I was hoping you knew someone."

"Does it have to be a pianist?"

"No. Not at all. You know someone?"

"Yes, as a matter of fact. A guitar player. Not everyone can afford him though. He's in demand because of his talent, so obviously his price will be much higher."

"How much we talking here?"

"Well—"

"You know what? It doesn't matter. He's hired. I don't want to take a chance. I'll freak out if I can't find someone. Tell him I want him."

"Well…you can tell him yourself."

"Fine."

He placed his hands in his hips and smiled.

"You?"

"Why not?"

She felt tears coming on. "You would do that for me?"

"Of course."

She charged forward and kissed him on the cheek. Then

she gave him a big hug. "You are amazing. Thank you!"

"My pleasure. But you still need to tell me you want me."

"Behave. You want another kick on the shins?"

He crinkled his nose. "Nah. I'll pass."

Natalie looked down and noticed he was still holding on to her after the hug. She looked up into his eyes and she saw something there. A sparkle. A kindness. A warmth. It felt more than just a hug from a friend. It felt intimate.

She stepped back and out of his arms. This had to be strictly business or she would lose control.

She placed her hands on her hips. Hopefully that would show more authority if the uniform didn't do it. "I'll let you play at my wedding under one condition."

"What's that?"

"I have to pay you the going rate for a wedding musician. Miguel charged me $500.00 for the ceremony. Is that acceptable to you?"

"No. It's not."

She stared at Giovanni for a moment. He wanted more money? She wasn't expecting that answer. "Okay, name your price."

"There is no price. My services are free. Consider it my gift to you."

"I told you I would only do it on one condition. That I pay you."

"And *I* am telling *you* that I will only do it on one condition —that you let me do it for free. Take it or leave it."

She let out a loud breath and tapped her foot on the floor. "You're stubborn."

Giovanni laughed. "Look in the mirror."

Natalie stuck her tongue out at Giovanni and smiled.

"When's the rehearsal?"

"Thursday at five, but you don't need to be there for that. I just need to know the length of the song so we can time out the processional."

"It's three minutes and thirty-five seconds, but that's probably going to be too long."

"Oh."

"I can do a custom version so it matches the timing of your walk down the aisle. I'll come to the rehearsal—it'll be easier that way. Plus it'll give me a chance to practice the song in a different setting."

She could tell, deep down, Giovanni was a good guy with a big heart. She was usually pretty good at reading people but was having a little bit of difficulty figuring out what his face was saying at the moment.

"Thank you" he said.

Thank you? Okay, maybe she had *a lot* of difficulty reading him.

She squished her eyebrows together. "What did I do?"

"You suggested that I call my ex and ask her why she didn't show up at the church."

"You did it?"

He nodded. "And she gave me an answer I wasn't

expecting."

"She's gay?"

"No! Why would you say that?"

She laughed. "Sorry, I couldn't help it. You were saying why she didn't show up…"

"She was afraid I wouldn't be able to support her type of lifestyle."

"A lifestyle of Louis Vuitton and Louboutins?"

"For starters, yes. She also had an issue with my mom. My mom's not a bad person and means well. She's just a tad obsessed with babies."

"Your mom is something, isn't she?"

"You know you also kissed her on the night of your bachelorette party?"

Natalie stared at Giovanni. She knew he was lying—there was no way she kissed his mom. Of course she had no way of knowing, but she could see that Giovanni had a slight grin on his face. She wasn't sure if she wanted to punch him or kick him this time.

She took a few more seconds to think about it and then let her fist fly into the side of his arm.

"Ouch!" said Giovanni, laughing. "You like to hit a lot, don't you?"

"You want another?"

"No! Man, you need to get laid." He jumped back and threw his hands up in the air. "Sorry! I didn't mean to say that. It just slipped out. Sorry. Really."

She spared him another punch since it was the truth. She *did* need to get laid.

But she wasn't going to tell him that.

Giovanni rubbed his arm. "Anyway, if you see my mother, run."

"Don't worry about me. I know how to deal with women like your mom."

"You think so?"

"I *know* so. I'm not easily intimidated."

Giovanni believed that. And she had a punch and a kick to prove it.

Natalie gave Giovanni her phone number and they agreed to talk the next day about the wedding music by phone or in person. Something felt very weird about that. Every day she saw him she was more convinced that she was marrying the wrong man.

Chapter Fourteen

The next day Natalie worked her beat downtown. It was an uneventful day. A couple of speeding tickets, three parking citations, and a disturbance at a boutique—two women fighting over a Versace blouse.

She had the urge to ask if one of them was Giovanni's ex, but she resisted.

It frustrated her that people fought over dumb things when there were more serious things happening in the world. Like weddings.

She thought about her life, her goals, and her upcoming marriage. She should be happier, but she wasn't. She had barely seen Jacks the last week except for the barbecue. But the one thing she couldn't shake from her thoughts were three words that Giovanni said.

Kissing is good!

She wondered what his kisses were like. And that's where the guilt came in. She should be thinking of Jacks' kisses, not Giovanni's. On the hike he mentioned he never saw the two of them kiss. When was her last passionate kiss with Jacks? When was the last time they went out and did something fun? And sex. What was that? Just the thought put her in a downer mood.

She arrived home, kissed Federico on the cheek, and headed to her room. She plopped down on the bed and sighed just as her phone rang. It was Jacks.

She rolled over on her back and stared at the ceiling. "Hi honey."

"Hey. Just checking in. How are things?"

Not good at all. "Good. Are you finally done with that case?"

"That's why I'm calling. We won! I want to go out tonight to celebrate."

She was happy for him, of course, but the last thing she wanted to do this evening was go out. She was tired and just wanted to throw on some comfy sweats and watch a movie. Preferably with some popcorn or a tub of chocolate chip cookie dough ice cream. "Can we celebrate in? Besides, we're going out tomorrow for the rehearsal dinner."

She didn't hear anything on the other end of the phone.

"Are you there?"

Jacks let a loud breath. "I'm here, but I can't believe you."

"What?"

"I've been working on this case for months. It's been the hardest thing I've ever done. Yes, I may be District Attorney soon, but I worked my ass off for it. All I want to do is celebrate out with my fiancée. Shouldn't we be celebrating our milestones and successes together? I took the liberty of making a reservation. I didn't expect you to be so indifferent."

"I'm not saying we shouldn't and I'm not indifferent at all. It's just…I'm tired."

She tried to think of the last time he let her decide on something to do. She liked a man who took charge and was decisive, but that didn't mean that she should lose the power to make any decisions at all. They were supposed to be a team.

What about my needs?

"Babe?" said Jacks.

"Yes."

"We can make it a short evening. Just a quick dinner and a toast, that's all I'm asking. Then we can go home and you can have a bowl of your favorite strawberry ice cream. I promise."

Strawberry? Seriously?

"Fine."

"We're going to that new Greek place. I'll pick you up in twenty minutes. I'm just going to dust off the car before I come over."

Of course.

So much for a relaxing evening.

*****

The hostess walked Giovanni, Danny, and Stevie to the booth in the corner. They sat and were handed menus. Giovanni ran his hands across the huge table—it had place settings for eight people. There were only three of them, so it seemed like a waste of space. What if a larger group came in? He would feel bad if they didn't have a table for them.

Giovanni held up his index finger to the hostess before she walked away. "Is there a smaller table available?"

The hostess looked to Stevie. "Oh. I thought—"

"No, no, no," said Stevie. "This will work. I'm…feeling a little claustrophobic this evening."

"Since when are you claustrophobic?"

"Since…I don't know. You know me. I've got many other undiscovered issues."

"Can't argue with that." He waved off the hostess. "Okay, I guess this will work. Thank you."

"My pleasure. Enjoy your meal."

Giovanni had wanted to try the new Greek place for the longest time. It was a pleasant surprise when Stevie and Danny called and said they were taking him there to celebrate his birthday.

He looked around the packed restaurant and nodded. "This place is popular." He set the menu on the table. "I really don't need to look at this. I'm having the moussaka. Read the rave reviews about it on Yelp."

Danny put his menu on top of Giovanni's. "Me too. Moussaka sounds tasty to me."

Stevie placed his menu on top of the pile. "Sounds like a plan, Charlie Chan."

"Moussaka is a weird word, isn't it?" said Danny. "I know

it's tasty. But it's weird."

"General Moussaka executed another fourteen men last night," said Stevie, trying to sound like a news reporter. "Film at eleven."

Giovanni just stared at Stevie. "I don't know where you get these things, but—"

"Hello son! Happy birthday!" Before Giovanni could respond, his mom and dad slid into the booth. "How's the birthday boy?"

"Fine." He gave Stevie the death stare. "I wasn't aware you were joining us."

"I wanted it to be a surprise," said Eleonora. "And by the look on your face I'd say it worked!"

That would be an understatement. He loved his parents. He knew there was probably a law somewhere stating that he had to. They're the ones who brought him into this world. Sure, he was grateful for that. But he could only handle his mother in small doses. And once she got on to the topic of grandchildren he wanted to kill her. He gave Stevie another look.

Stevie shrugged. "I wanted to say something but you know how persuasive your mom can be."

Eleonora gestured to Stevie. "I do recall you happily agreeing to keeping this a secret."

"Ha! You said if I didn't keep the secret you would detach my testicles, blend them with soy milk and strawberries, and make me drink it."

Giovanni stared at his mother. He could picture her saying that.

"You know how Stevie can exaggerate!" she said. "Come on, I *did not* say soy milk."

Giovanni didn't believe her and continued to stare at her.

"It was almond milk, actually. There *is* a difference."

Right. He prayed that his mother would behave and that they would be able to have a peaceful meal. He didn't want any more surprises.

They ordered their meals and were enjoying drinks when Stevie pointed to a table nearby. "Hey Giovanni, look. It's Federico's granddaughter. What's her name again?"

Giovanni turned so fast he almost pulled a muscle in his neck. "Natalie."

Natalie and Jacks were being seated at a table across the way.

"The drunk fertile one," said Eleonora. "You need to marry that woman and make babies since you didn't even consider Choo as a viable option." She pointed to Natalie. "What is she doing with that loser?"

Giovanni raised an eyebrow. "You know that guy?"

"Of course. He's the hotshot attorney who just sent some mafia guy to prison. It was all over the news...though his name escapes me at the moment."

"Jacks Cole," said Giovanni.

"Right. More like Ass Hole. That guy takes on high-profile cases for the exposure so he can move up. He doesn't do it because he cares about the people. He makes a lot of money." She took a sip of her wine. "Probably to compensate for his tiny cock."

"Mom, please."

"I just call it like I see it. You need to go over there and show that woman your penis. It's big, powerful, and ready to give me grandchildren. Be proud."

"Have you ever heard of the expression 'ladylike'?"

"Don't you go acting like I don't know about the size of your penis. I remember *very well* that growth spurt you had in junior high when you came down with that disgusting case of jock itch. Who had to spray your balls? Me, that's who. Shouldn't be a surprise, your girth, really. You got that from your father." She smiled proudly and patted the top of Alfonso's hand. "Good boy."

"Enough, Eleonora." Alfonso finally found his voice.

"But as you can see, your father has lost his balls, so I guess it all balances out in the end."

Giovanni scratched the top of his hand and his mom noticed.

Shit.

He wasn't going to tell her about the hike with Natalie or the fact that they both had poison oak. The last thing he wanted to do was give his mother hope that something would happen with the two of them.

Even though Giovanni wished something would happen.

Eleonora pointed to his hand. "You got jock itch on your

hands now?"

He slid his hands under the table. "It's nothing."

Giovanni stared across the restaurant at Natalie. Even from there he could see she was looking lovelier than ever. No way he could go talk to her though. Jacks would be able to read him like a book. He never was very good at hiding his feelings and he had feelings for Natalie. Truth be told, he wished she wasn't marrying Jacks. It didn't seem fair. And to top it off, who volunteered to play the music for the ceremony?

Me. The idiot.

Giovanni felt conflicted and needed to see her. Up close. "I need to slide out of the booth."

Eleonora gestured in the direction of Natalie. "You going to go show her who has the balls?"

"No, Mom, I'm not. I'm going to go use the bathroom."

"Of course. You need to tidy up first. Good call."

He slid out of the booth after Eleonora and Alfonso.

The restrooms were located right behind Natalie's table. Just a little peek, that's all.

Jacks' back was to Giovanni. Perfect. He neared her table as she chatted with Jacks. She didn't look very happy.

Natalie looked up, caught a glimpse of Giovanni, and froze.

Jacks turned around, but Giovanni hid behind the nude statue of *Discobolus* before he could be seen. Then he snuck into the bathroom and washed his hands. They itched even more with the hot water.

What the hell am I doing? This is stupid.

He opened the bathroom door to head back to his table. The food would probably be there when he got back. As he came out of the bathroom he turned and ran straight into Natalie. He knocked her over the bench into a fake pomegranate tree.

"Oh God," said Giovanni, reaching down to help her up.

She brushed off her dress and let out a deep breath. "You trying to kill me?"

"Sorry! What are you doing standing so close to the men's restroom?"

"Never mind that." She pursed her lips. "Did you follow me here?"

"I got here first and I saw you when you came in. *You* must be following *me*."

"I am *not* following you." She scratched the top of her hand.

Giovanni pointed to her hand. "What's wrong?" He knew what was wrong, but he wanted to see if she would admit it.

"You know what's wrong because you gave it to me."

"I gave it to *you*? Come on! You were the one who pushed me in the bushes."

Natalie poked him in the chest. "You said you got to first base with me!"

"I *did* get to first base with you! But you initiated it!"

An older woman passed between the two of them to enter

the bathroom. She kept her head down and grinned. She'd obviously heard him and was trying to be discreet. The woman disappeared into the bathroom.

"I initiated it?" asked Natalie.

"Yes."

"You're not making this up?"

"No. You kissed me."

She stood there in a daze.

Giovanni shrugged. "And I liked it. Even though it was a little sloppy."

"Sloppy? Wait a minute…you liked it?"

He nodded.

She looked up at Giovanni and her gaze drifted to his mouth again.

He wished she would quit doing that. He so wanted to kiss her. Not a sloppy kiss. Not a kiss initiated by her. He wanted to be in control and kiss her good. Right now.

But it wasn't going to happen. And he was just torturing himself thinking about it.

"Hello, Miss Fertile," said Eleonora. "Has my son shown you his penis yet? It's large. Very, *very* large."

"Stop it, Mom."

Eleonora ignored him and moved closer to Natalie. "We should talk sometime. Can I take you out to lunch?"

"No, Mom! Enough is enough."

"How could it be enough when I just started?"

"Leave Natalie alone."

Natalie waved Giovanni off. "Don't worry about me. I can take care of myself." She glanced down at Giovanni's zipper region.

Why the hell is she looking down there?

Natalie shook her head at Eleonora. "I think your son is too much of a man for me. I wouldn't be able to handle it."

Oh. Nice play. And of course Giovanni's ego was happy.

Eleonora pointed a finger at Natalie. "Don't sell yourself short. I'm a good judge of character and I can see you've got what it takes to be with him."

"I had considered it until you came along."

Eleonora cocked her head to the side. "What do you mean?"

"I think it's time I played for the other team."

Huh? Was she really going there?

Giovanni was slapped in the head with that one. He wanted to laugh. His lips quivered, trying to hold it in.

Eleonora eyed Natalie for a moment and then took a step back. "I'm not sure I understand what you mean."

"Oh, I think you do."

Eleonora fidgeted with her sleeve. "I…need to get back. The food must be getting cold."

Natalie rubbed the side of Eleonora's arm. "It was *such* a pleasure seeing you. I mean, *really.*"

And just like that Eleonora was gone.

Natalie and Giovanni shared a laugh together

Giovanni bowed to her. "You are amazing."

"Thank you. That was fun."

"Yeah."

Natalie stared at his lips and then shook her head like she had water in her ear. "I need to get back."

"Of course. But tell me something…"

She bit her lower lip. Giovanni loved when she did that.

"If you were single right now, which I know you're not… But if you were…would you go out with me?"

Natalie didn't answer. She turned a nice shade of pink and bit her lower lip again. "Let's not do this. I should go. We need to talk about the wedding music soon, okay?"

"Yes, we do. As well as other things more personal."

She turned and ran straight into the chest of Jacks. He did not look happy either.

"Where have you been?" said Jacks. "The appetizers have been sitting on the table." He gave Giovanni the evil eye. "What is *he* doing here?"

"Hi Jacks." Giovanni held out his hand and Jacks left him hanging there.

Dick.

Giovanni had a cruel thought. Jacks could shake his hand, get his poison oak, go home, jerk off, and then get the poison oak on his—

"Never mind," said Jacks. He took Natalie by the hand and practically dragged her back to her table. As she walked away she glanced back at Giovanni and smiled.

What did she mean by that smile?

He wasn't sure, but he would never complain about a smile like that.

When Giovanni arrived back to the booth Stevie, Danny, and his mom were holding up shot glasses of Ouzo. Alfonso just sat back and watched since he didn't drink.

"Opa!" they all yelled and slammed their shots. Without him.

Giovanni raised his palms in the air. "I guess it's not necessary for the man of honor to be here for the celebration?"

"You snoozo, no Ouzo!" said Stevie.

Giovanni and Alfonso were the only ones not laughing.

He glanced back at Natalie. For someone who was getting married she sure had a long face. She sat there with her chin on her hands as Jacks talked on his cell phone.

Eleonora and Alfonso got out of the booth and let Giovanni slide back in. He popped the last piece of spanakopita in his mouth. As Stevie went on and on about Michael Jackson and his theory of why he only wore one glove, Giovanni pulled out his cell phone and held it in his hand under the table for a moment.

He had the urge to text Natalie.

To say something that would make her laugh, smile, or at least cheer her up a little. Maybe she didn't have her phone with her or maybe she wouldn't see the text until she got home. That was okay. If she didn't get it now, she would get it later. He cared about her and wanted her to feel better.

He also wanted to flirt with her.

He glanced down at his phone and texted Natalie:

I get a kick out of you.

He pressed *send* and looked up to see if she would make a move for the purse to get her phone. She stared at Jacks who was still talking on his cell. What was with that guy? Could he not see that amazing creature in front of him?

Come on, get your phone.

Maybe it was too noisy in the restaurant for her to hear the phone. He continued to watch her. Finally she turned to her side and grabbed her purse from the other chair.

Yes! We have lift off!

She pulled out the phone and read it. She paused, met his gaze, and then dropped her head down. Was she responding to him? Giovanni couldn't see her fingers moving since they were under her table.

Reply! You can do it! Say something!

A few seconds later Giovanni's phone vibrated. Natalie had responded.

Don't make me come over there and demonstrate.

Giovanni laughed.

Danny, Stevie, Eleonora, and Alfonso stopped talking and looked in his direction.

"You know you sound like a dolphin sometimes when you laugh?" said Stevie.

"Why did you do that?" said Giovanni.

"What?"

"Talk about animals, that's what. You trying to get Danny going?" He pointed to Danny and said, "Please don't tell us about dolphins and their mating habits. I can see the wheels turning in your head. Just shut the engine down."

Danny ignored him. "Dolphins sleep with one eye open and have retractable penises."

"Here we go again…"

"And ravenous sexual appetites. They have no problem humping inanimate objects."

Stevie slapped Giovanni on the back. "You must be part dolphin!"

Once again everyone was laughing at the table but Giovanni. He got distracted when the food arrived. He took a couple of bites of his moussaka and took a peek at Natalie who was now eating. And her loser of the year fiancé was still on the phone. Giovanni typed another text to Natalie.

You look bored.

A few seconds later he got a text.

Out of my skull.

He quickly typed another message to her:

Meet me by the bathrooms again.

A few seconds later.

No way.

No way? He wasn't expecting that answer. He was probably just as bored as she was and was hoping for another fun rendezvous with that spunky, beautiful cop. He loved Stevie and Danny, but they didn't act like themselves when they were in the presence of Eleonora. Not the greatest birthday celebration in the world, really. But he wasn't going to take no for an answer from Natalie.

Giovanni tapped the side of his mother's leg. "Let me out again."

Alfonso and Eleonora slid out of the booth, followed by Giovanni.

Eleonora eyed him suspiciously. "You just went to the bathroom."

Giovanni faked a smile. "You know I have to pee more than usual when I get excited."

He walked in the direction of the bathrooms and stood behind the statue of *Discobolus* again. Giovanni knew his body could be seen from Natalie's side, but his head was completely hidden by the discus in *Discobolus'* hand. He slowly peeked from around the discus and discovered Natalie staring straight at him.

She gave him a what-the-hell-are-you-doing look.

He pointed his head in the direction of the bathrooms a couple of times and she mouthed the word "no" to him.

Giovanni mouthed the word "yes" to her.

He didn't wait for a response this time. He slid to the side and took a few more steps until he was standing in between the men's and women's restrooms in front of a giant hanging canvas depicting The Parthenon.

What was he going to say to her this time? He had no clue. In fact, he had no idea what the hell he was doing. All he knew was that a force was moving him to be closer to Natalie. How could he have feelings for a woman so quickly?

Again…no clue.

He paced back and forth in front of The Parthenon. Surely she was going to join him there. She knew he was waiting, so what was taking her so long? He pulled out his phone and texted her:

Chicken.

Fifteen seconds later Natalie walked toward him.

She stopped and stood there with her hands on her hips. "Chicken? Ha!"

He smiled. "Well…you proved me wrong."

"This is crazy."

He couldn't argue with that, but his friends and his own mother accused him of having no balls. Time to make some changes. He liked her. A lot.

He moved a step closer to her. "I just wanted to ask you something."

"You were doing pretty well with the texting earlier. Why the face-to-face?"

"I like your face."

She bit her bottom lip.

"And the rest of you."

"Okay."

"So, let me ask you. Is this thing you have with Jacks, this relationship, what you want for the rest of your life?"

She let out a deep breath. "Why are you here? And why are you doing this to me?"

"What?"

"Putting doubts in my head."

So she had doubts. Not a surprise, but he had nothing to do with them.

"I'm not putting doubts in your head. They were there before I ever came along. And the reason I am here is because it's my birthday and my friends wanted to take me out to celebrate. Do you think it's a coincidence that you showed up at the same restaurant?"

"So you think we were supposed to see each other tonight?"

He nodded.

"I wish I would have known it was your birthday,—it would have been the perfect excuse not to be here with Jacks and his phone."

"Well, if I had invited you and you had accepted you still would be here. But the reason why I didn't invite you is I didn't know my friends were planning a surprise party for me."

She smiled and shrugged. "Happy birthday." She stepped forward and hugged him and held on longer than he thought she would. And he had no problem with that. And why did she always have to smell so good? The name of her perfume had to be *Drive Giovanni Crazy*.

Damn, she felt good too.

He wasn't sure if that was her heart or his that was banging like that. Maybe it was both.

Natalie kissed him on the cheek.

He *so* wanted to move his mouth over a little so their lips connected. He knew there would be fireworks if he did. He knew she felt something for him. It was obvious.

But was it enough for her to cancel her wedding?

She pulled away. "You're driving me crazy."

Giovanni grinned. "I was about to accuse you of the same thing."

Natalie sighed. "What am I doing?" She shook her head. "This is wrong. And it has to stop."

Then she turned and walked away.

Chapter Fifteen

Giovanni drove through the gates of Thousand Castles Winery and parked. He was running late, but hopefully everyone was too busy with wedding-related things to notice.

He felt conflicted playing music for a wedding he did not believe in. Natalie didn't belong with Jacks.

She belongs with me.

Still there was no way he would cancel playing for the ceremony. Federico was a good friend and his granddaughter was possibly the woman of Giovanni's dreams. At least he could see Natalie one more time before she walked the plank.

He grabbed his guitar from the back seat, closed the car door, and walked by Jacks' car in the parking lot. The Camaro occupied two parking spaces.

Why do people do that?

He continued toward the ceremony area deep in thought. Would he say something to Natalie? And if so, what would it be? He certainly wouldn't have any privacy with her. Federico would be there and many others. Including Jacks.

The first person Giovanni saw was Federico.

"Giovanni," said Federico. "Natalie is looking for you. Are you ready to play music for the most beautiful granddaughter in the world?"

"I'm looking forward to it," Giovanni lied.

"Great!"

It was like Federico never had a bad day—he was amazing. How could a person stay so positive all the time? Especially when his granddaughter was going to marry someone who was not meant for her.

Giovanni rubbed the back of his neck. "Can I ask you something?"

"Of course."

"I think you and I both know this marriage is not a good thing. Why don't you do something?"

Federico nodded. "Ahh. Well…" He smiled. "I guess I could ask you the same question, now couldn't I?"

Giovanni didn't answer.

Federico put his hand on Giovanni's shoulder. "Things always have a way of working out. She will have her happy ending just like I did. Excuse me—I need to get my glasses from the car so I can see!"

"Of course."

The guy was amazing.

Hopefully Natalie had some of that good energy that Federico had and was calm and peaceful.

Maybe she wouldn't even notice the time!

"Finally!" said Natalie. "You trying to drive me crazy?"

So much for hoping.

"I'm very sorry," said Giovanni. "I'm ready to go."

"Jacks is in the bathroom and my grandfather just went to get his glasses, so we'll start in a moment. This is Rebecca, my matron of honor."

Giovanni smiled at Rebecca. "Natalie was pretty hammered that night so it's understandable she forgot we've already met. She doesn't even remember she kissed me."

Rebecca's mouth hung open. "She never said anything to me about kissing you!"

Natalie smacked Giovanni on the arm and looked toward the restroom. "Shh! This is not the time for that. You trying to get me to go Zilla on you?"

Giovanni laughed. "No. That would be scary."

Natalie turned to Rebecca. "The wedding coordinator is giving me the evil eye. Can you go see what she wants?"

Rebecca glanced over to the wedding coordinator, then back to Natalie. "Fine. But we need to talk about that kiss later."

Rebecca walked away and Giovanni leaned into Natalie. "You still sure you want to go through with this? You could marry me instead."

"Don't start. Not now. Stress gives me pimples and I will kill you if I have a pimple on my wedding day. Do you want to die?"

"Not particularly."

She was so cute when she was nervous. His gaze dropped to her feet. She was barefoot for some reason. Her toenails were painted purple this time. Not a surprise.

Giovanni pointed to her feet. "Cute toes."

"Thank you. And quit being nice. The shoes were killing me."

Giovanni nodded. "There was a movie around five years ago—I think it was with Jennifer Aniston."

Natalie crossed her arms. "We're talking about movies now?"

"*He's Just Not That Into You.* That was the name of it, I think. Do you remember that movie?"

"I remember it but I didn't see it. What's your point?"

"Well, I didn't see it either. But my point is…you are living that movie. *You* are going to marry a man who's just not that into you. And I don't think you're into him that much either."

"You don't know what you're talking about."

"I'm pretty sure I do. Can't you see there's no passion in your relationship? Does he know your favorite color is purple or that you bite your lower lip when you're nervous?"

She bit her lower lip. "I—"

"I doubt it. He may be some big time lawyer, but he doesn't notice the little details in your relationship. Does he know that we both have poison oak on the same hand and that we got it when we went on a hike together?"

"Uh…"

"No. He doesn't. And if he did find out he wouldn't care! I'll tell you what, if I found out my fiancée went on a hike with another man and didn't tell me I would go ballistic. And

Jacks wouldn't."

"I wouldn't *what?*" asked Jacks.

"Nothing," said Natalie.

Giovanni held out the top of his red, irritated hand so Jacks could see it. "I was asking Natalie if you would recognize that I had poison oak on my hand."

Jacks leaned in to get a better look at his hand. "That's poison oak?"

"Yes. And Natalie has it too. On the same hand."

Jacks turned to look at her hand. "Is that right?"

Natalie nodded and held out her hand but didn't answer.

"How did you both get poison oak?"

"Natalie and I went on a hike the other night," said Giovanni. "Just the two of us."

Natalie moved her hand behind her back. "You were working late that night. Remember?"

Jacks shook his finger at Natalie. "I'm really disappointed with you."

"You are?"

"Of course. You need to put something on that hand. That's contagious. And I could get it too!" He waved to get the attention of the wedding coordinator. "Okay, let's get rolling so we're not late for dinner."

Giovanni leaned into Natalie. "Told you."

Natalie didn't answer.

Everyone took their places for the ceremony. Giovanni sat down in the chair, made a few adjustments to the guitar, and waited for the coordinator's cue. Natalie peeked over at Giovanni and quickly looked away.

Smooth. She was a good cop but could never be a spy.

Giovanni took a deep breath and admired the view of the valley. It was a gorgeous day, but he could see some clouds moving in slowly. Was there a storm on the way? Maybe that would be the sign that her marriage would be doomed. Rain on her wedding day. Oh, who was he kidding? He wasn't superstitious like that.

The pastor stood just a few feet away at the altar with Jacks.

A few minutes later the wedding coordinator gave Giovanni the hand signal and he started playing. He watched as the bridal party walked down the aisle. Then Natalie approached, escorted by Federico.

Beautiful Natalie.

The woman was getting married but couldn't summon enough energy to put a smile on her face?

That's a red flag! I should know! I'm the king of red flags!

The more Giovanni thought about it the more it pissed him off. He continued to play the song until she reached the altar at the front.

The pastor filled everyone in on what would happen along with the help of the wedding coordinator. Everything seemed to run pretty smoothly up until then.

The pastor turned to Jacks. "And then after the vows I'll say, 'You may kiss your wife.' And that is your cue for the big kiss before I present you to everyone."

"You should practice the kiss," said one of the bridesmaids.

Please don't.

Natalie bit her lower lip. "That's not necessary, really."

Rebecca frowned. It looked like she didn't believe in this marriage either.

"Great idea," said Jacks.

There the man went again, not listening to what Natalie wanted.

Jacks pulled on Natalie's ear like he was trying to milk a cow. God. Was that supposed to be romantic? Therapeutic maybe, but not romantic!

Jacks leaned and—

"Ouch!" said Natalie.

Jacks looked down at her feet. "Sorry, I didn't realize you were barefoot."

Of course you didn't notice, you idiot.

Natalie winced in pain. "That's okay. The pain will go away."

Jacks stepped forward again and kissed her.

It was the most passionless kiss in the history of the world. Too bad Guinness was not here to document it.

No tongue. No emotion. No passion. He didn't even close his eyes.

What the hell was that?

Absolutely pathetic.

"Perfect!" said the pastor.

Perfect?

Obviously he was blind.

"Wait a minute!" yelled Giovanni.

He couldn't take it anymore and was about to do something he might regret. His heart rate sped up as he stood and leaned his guitar against his chair. Time to get this off his chest. This was where he exposed the fraud that was their relationship. He was going to tell Natalie how he felt. He had never felt so confident and alive. She would see that they had a million things more in common than she did with Jacks. It was like Giovanni had ten shots of espresso.

Let's do this!

"No, no, no, no, no," Giovanni said, pushing Jacks aside. "That was not a kiss! *This* is a kiss!"

He grabbed Natalie by the waist and kissed her. And he kissed her damn good. She moaned, a good sign, so he deepened the kiss. Giovanni felt the poke of a finger on his back but didn't care. Natalie was an angel and there was no way in hell he was going to let her marry Jacks.

Jacks cleared his throat. "Hey!"

Giovanni felt the pokes get stronger on his back. Natalie broke free from the kiss and moved a step back from Giovanni, not speaking.

She looked at Jacks.

Then Giovanni.

Jacks.

Giovanni.

It was like she was watching a tennis match.

Then Giovanni watched in slow motion as Natalie's hand came flying around to make contact with his face.

She slapped him good. Hard.

He stood there for a few seconds wondering what just happened.

Did she just slap me? Hell yeah, she did! But why?

Giovanni held the side of his face. "I don't get it. We have a connection—there's something between us, I know it." She still didn't say a word. "You felt something—admit it."

She stood there. Silent.

"Admit it!"

"Please leave!" she yelled. "And don't bother coming to the wedding tomorrow."

He turned his palms up. "But…you kissed me back."

Giovanni felt the hand of Jacks spin him around and before he could react he was knocked to the ground by a fist to the face. Jacks might be a passionless man when it came to Natalie, but the guy knew how to hit. Very well.

Giovanni's ears were ringing and his face was throbbing. But it was odd because he didn't feel any pain. He'd read somewhere that kisses had endorphins and were natural pain relievers. Could it be? It didn't really matter. What mattered was…they kissed.

And what an *amazing* kiss it was!

Jacks stood over Giovanni as he lay on the ground, his

hand covering his eye. "You heard her. Get out of here. You're fired."

Fired? Who are you? Donald Trump?

How pathetic was that? He got fired from a volunteer position.

Giovanni didn't say another word. He got up and looked around at all of the people staring at him. The always-happy Federico didn't very look happy at all. In fact, he looked away.

Giovanni brushed off his pants, grabbed his guitar, and made his way to his car. It was one of the longest walks of his life. During the walk his mind was kind enough to torture him with the same thought over and over again.

She kissed me back. She kissed me back.

*****

Natalie didn't say a word in the car. Neither did Jacks. Giovanni would not be a part of their wedding day. She closed her eyes. She really couldn't believe what had happened.

What the hell was Giovanni thinking? Kissing her in front of everyone? In front of her fiancé? Yes, the kiss was amazing. But wrong place, wrong time.

Heck, wrong lifetime.

When they arrived at the restaurant for the rehearsal dinner, Natalie went straight to the bathroom. Jacks joined the others in the private dining room in the back.

She stared at herself in the mirror.

What a nightmare.

Yes, Giovanni was right, she kissed him back. It was the best kiss of her life.

But it was wrong. Very wrong.

Maybe if she had met Giovanni six months ago or last year, there could have been a chance between them. But what was she supposed to do now? Cancel the wedding? Not show up? How did she know it wasn't just lust or physical attraction?

Giovanni got jilted twice. That would be too much of a weird, freaky coincidence if she did the same thing to Jacks.

"Not gonna happen."

Rebecca obviously had Natalie on her radar. She entered the bathroom.

"Wow," said Rebecca, hugging Natalie. "I really couldn't say anything at the rehearsal, but that was like something out of a movie. Like in *The Runaway Bride*, remember the scene where Richard Gere kissed Julia Roberts in the church? Then he gets punched by her jock football coach fiancé?"

Natalie forced a smile. "Believe me, I thought of the same thing."

"The difference is...*you* didn't leave with Richard Gere."

"And I made the right choice."

"Did you?"

"Yes! Jacks would make a good husband."

"And?"

"And what?"

"There's got to be more than that."

Natalie sighed. "Honestly? I am happy with that. And if you are going to suggest that there's something going on between me and Giovanni, forget it."

She wasn't sure why she lied.

"I saw something," said Rebecca.

"No, you didn't. And there's no sure thing with Giovanni, anyway. Sure, he's sweet and kind and—"

"Gorgeous."

She nodded. "Yeah, he's gorgeous. But there's no guarantee with him."

"And there is with Jacks?"

"Yes! I mean…no, there's no guarantee. I'm just saying…" She took a deep breath. "I don't want to end up like your Aunt Jean."

"Oh…"

Rebecca's Aunt, Jean was the pickiest woman Natalie knew. And not so coincidentally, the loneliest. She kept waiting for the perfect man to arrive but everyone knew there was no such thing. Everyone except Jean. Now she was just an old, bitter, lonely woman.

"I don't want to be alone."

Rebecca rubbed Natalie on her back and smiled. "*You* will never be alone. You are one of the most amazing, wonderful people I know. You care so much about everyone, even strangers! That's a certain quality most people don't have. And I'm jealous of the way guys look at you. Especially Giovanni."

"Thanks, but let's forget about him."

"You really think it's going to be that easy to forget about him?"

No. It wasn't going to be easy at all. Giovanni was a special man and, yes, she had feelings for him. But the embarrassment she would feel from canceling the wedding would haunt her. How would she be able to look at her friends and co-workers in the eyes after that? Too much has gone into this wedding planning and she did not want to look like a failure.

What if you make the wrong decision and your marriage is a failure? Isn't that going to look worse?

"Oh, shut up!" yelled Natalie.

Rebecca stared at Natalie. "Sorry."

"Not you! So sorry!" She hugged Rebecca and kissed her on the cheek. "I was talking to my mind."

"Tell your mind to take a hike. Follow your heart."

That's what Federico had been telling her all along. The doubts crept back into her head and she tried to shake them off. It was time for the rehearsal dinner and she needed to concentrate on that.

"Let's go join the others."

"Are you sure you know what you're doing?"

"Absolutely not. But let's not let that get in our way of

enjoying a wonderful meal this evening."

Time to focus on the present and forget about Giovanni.

She needed to try. She was going to marry Jacks. He was a good man. And she would keep telling herself that for the rest of the evening until she was convinced.

Chapter Sixteen

"Son of a Bigfoot!"

Giovanni sat up in his bed and gently felt his cheek. He had just rolled over in his sleep and turned directly on the left side of his face where he was pretty sure he was getting a black eye. It hurt like hell.

Precious jumped up and walked from the foot of the bed to Giovanni's pillow and licked him on his chin. Sweet dog.

Precious somehow knew that Giovanni wasn't feeling well. Better licking him on his chin than his eye, which was throbbing.

A black eye courtesy of Jacks Cole.

Idiot.

Giovanni was actually thinking of himself.

What was he thinking kissing Natalie there like that? It was like he had a testosterone imbalance and wanted to conquer the woman like a caveman. Then what was he going to do? Carry her back to his cave where he would grunt a few times, make a fire by rubbing two sticks together, and make babies on the dirt floor?

Caveman!

Any chance he had with the woman was now gone. What

a shame. He liked her a hundred times more than his last fiancée—a thousand even. Maybe he even loved her.

"Shut your mouth!"

Precious ducked her head and walked back to the foot of the bed with her tail between her legs. She laid her chin on top of her paws, her sweet eyes staring back at Giovanni.

"No, no, not you, Precious. I'm talking to myself." He sat up and petted her along the length of her body. "Sorry I startled you. It's just…I was an idiot, you know? Of course you do, dogs are smart. Smarter than humans, that's for sure."

"Arf!"

"Hey, you don't have to rub it in my face. I know you have some intelligence!"

"Arf!"

Maybe she wasn't answering him, but politely asking if she could go to the bathroom.

"Do you have to go pee?"

"Arf!"

Precious jumped off the bed and ran out of the room.

"That answers that question."

Giovanni slid out of bed and went to the side door where Precious was patiently waiting. He let her out and she ran to the back to do her business. He stood there watching her. She was a cool dog.

He wouldn't mind being a dog right about now. Dogs were cool in general. Simple, loyal creatures. Just happy with some food in the belly, a place to sleep, and a toy or two.

Speaking of Precious, what the hell happened to Beatrice? Giovanni had tried calling her a few times but it went straight to voicemail.

How come she hadn't contacted him? She should be back by now, shouldn't she? Giovanni guessed it didn't matter. He was becoming rather attached to Precious and was okay watching her longer.

"Buon giorno, Giovanni! Another day with no pants is a good day, no?"

Giovanni looked down and realized he was standing there in his underwear again. He slowly backed behind the garbage can, his usual move.

Did Federico ever have a bad day? After what had happened yesterday you'd think the guy would be mad at Giovanni. Not even close. All of his teeth were happily on display.

"I'm sorry, Federico. I'm sure I embarrassed you yesterday. I don't know what came over me."

"I do."

'You do?"

"Yes! You were under the influence of my beautiful granddaughter!"

Giovanni nodded. Federico was a smart man.

"Would you believe me if I told you it happened to me too?"

"What? Somebody punched you in the face?"

"Yes!"

"Why are you so excited about being punched in the face?"

Federico laughed. "*That* is how I met my wife, Olive!"

"Okay, I've got to hear this one. Maybe I should put on some pants or something."

"Pants are not necessary—this will only take a minute!"

Federico always had some amazing stories, but he was also known to embellish things on occasion.

Precious returned from her pee and Giovanni picked her up and scratched her on the head. "Please. Tell me the story."

"I was a young man in Roma, barely eighteen years old, taking a picture in front of La Fontana de Trevi. I heard a man talking disrespectfully to a woman—men were always known for whistling and flirting with the women in Italy— that has not changed. But this man took it too far and I could tell the woman felt scared and uncomfortable. I asked him to leave her alone and he did not say one single word to me! He simply hit me and knocked me into the fountain. And this is the most amazing part—Olive got into the water to help me out!"

Giovanni smiled and set Precious back on the ground. "That's a great story. What happened after that?"

Federico smiled. "We fell in love, decided to come to America, and took the maiden voyage of the largest cruise ship in the world to New York."

"That was rather adventurous of you."

He nodded. "But we almost didn't make it! Four days into the cruise the ship hit an iceberg and—"

"What?"

"Yes, yes, it was amazing. Many people lost their lives and —"

"Nice try!" said Giovanni, laughing. "That was *Titanic*."

Federico grinned. "I thought I could get you on that one."

"Come on, everyone has seen *Titanic*. But the first part of the story was true, right?"

He nodded. "One hundred percent."

"You always knew she was the one for you after the fountain?"

"Always."

Giovanni thought about it for a moment. "How did you know?"

Federico placed his palm on his chest. "I followed my heart. That is it, nothing more. Always follow your heart. It will never lead you down the wrong path."

Giovanni pointed to his eye. "See this? It's from following my heart."

Federico held up his index finger. "Ah, but are you still following it?"

"Why? So I can get the other eye to match this one? My heart led me down the wrong path."

"No, my friend. You may have encountered a slight detour. Keep following it. Your heart is better than a GPS!"

230

Giovanni laughed and saw something move in the kitchen window of Federico's house. He looked up and spotted Natalie staring straight at him. This would be the *second* time she saw him in his underwear in the side yard. She was going to really think he was an exhibitionist and arrest him.

Federico turned to follow Giovanni's eyes but Natalie was gone. He turned back and smiled. "Okay, you follow your heart. And *I* will follow my stomach back to the house for breakfast."

Breakfast sounded good. After Giovanni fed Precious and ate he worked in his guitar studio for a few hours. It was a good distraction and he enjoyed it immensely until his phone rang. He put the glue down and checked the caller ID. It was his mother and he decided to answer the call. He could try to avoid her, but she would just come over unannounced.

"Hi Mom, I'm kind of busy at the moment. Can I call you later?"

"You are never too busy for your mom. Mrs. Stanton said she saw you at Whole Foods with a black eye. Are you gang-bangin' now?"

"Yes, Mom. I needed to find a new hobby ever since I stopped robbing banks. Hangin' with my homies and poppin' caps in people's asses is what I live for."

"This is not funny. At least tell me you are sleeping with the fertile one."

"She's getting married tomorrow."

"So that was the truth?"

"Of course it was the truth!"

Giovanni heard his mother breathing but she wasn't speaking.

"Mom?"

"Where is she getting married?"

"Thousand Castles Winery. Why?"

"Obviously there's something going on between the two of you. You need to get down to that winery and stop the wedding."

"I'm not going to stop the wedding."

"I want grandchildren! Do you hear me?"

Giovanni rolled his eyes. "Yes, Mom. It's the same old story."

"If you don't stop the wedding, I will!"

"Don't you even think about it! Hey…the call is breaking up and—"

Giovanni disconnected the call and set the phone down. This was not the first time he had hung up on his mother and it probably wouldn't be the last. He used to feel guilty about it but not anymore.

A few seconds later it rang again but he let it go to voicemail. It felt good to have some peace and quiet.

He reached down to rub Precious on the belly. "You're a good girl and you never tell me what to do." She stretched and moaned as he continued to rub her. "Oh, you like that, do you?"

"Oh yes," said Stevie. "Give it to me, baby."

"Give it To Me Baby was recorded by Rick James," said Danny, entering the studio right behind Stevie. "1981."

Stevie twirled his finger in the air. "Big whoopdy doo. Tell someone who cares."

Precious ran to greet the boys and Giovanni turned around. "What are you guys up to?"

"Jesus!" yelled Stevie, pointing at his black eye like it was a monster. "What happened to you? Did you fall over while trying to hump an inanimate object?" Stevie held out a high-five for Danny who didn't reciprocate.

Giovanni shook his head. Should he tell them? If he did he wouldn't hear the end of it. But if he didn't tell them they wouldn't leave him alone until he did. Basically he was screwed either way.

"I kissed Natalie at her wedding rehearsal and her fiancé hit me."

Giovanni wished he had something to put into both of Stevie and Danny's open mouths. Maybe a couple of guitar picks? No. Something bigger. A banana, maybe. Why were they so surprised?

Stevie held up a high-five for Giovanni. "You got your balls back. Yes!"

Giovanni stared at his hand in the air.

Stevie slowly brought his hand back down and frowned. "Doesn't anybody high-five anymore? What else can guys share? We can't go to the bathroom together."

"Ignore him," said Danny. "Tell us about the girl. Did you

get her?"

"She chose him."

"That doesn't make any sense. How was the kiss?"

He smiled. "The best. And she kissed me back."

"No!"

"Yes."

"You rocked it!" said Stevie. "I knew you would because I have to say you've got a nice tongue, Giovanni. Smooth. Perfectly proportioned to your mouth. A nice hue as well. Do you use a tongue scraper after you brush?"

Danny and Giovanni stared at Stevie.

"What?"

They continued to stare.

Stevie reached down to pet Precious. "Hey, you know I'm not gay so quit looking at me that way! I just notice certain things and I believe in cleanliness and hygiene." Precious licked Stevie's hand and he pulled away and stared at it. "Where has this dog's mouth been? Never mind! I don't wanna know. Anyway, what was I saying? Oh yeah, the kiss. I'm telling you…it ain't over."

"Yes, it is."

"Not even close. If she kissed you back you're still in the game, my man. I've got books to back up my statements!"

"She's getting married! She told me to take a hike then she slapped me. End of story."

"That was just for show. She digs you and you need to go over there and stop that wedding."

"You sound like my mom."

Like he was going to stop the wedding. Wouldn't it be easier just to go next door and talk with her? Less dramatic, that's for sure. He had been a part of two almost-weddings and they were humiliating. And who knew, maybe he would get punched again. This time by Natalie. She took it easy on him with that slap. And with those kicks. She was a cop and could have easily broken one or both of his kneecaps.

No. Not gonna happen.

Stevie pushed Giovanni. "You're thinking too much. Do you like the girl or not?"

"Yes, but—"

"Do it. Get the girl. We'll go with you for emotional support. You be the balls and we'll be the sac."

"Sometimes you're not very eloquent with words."

"Damn skippy, Mr. Pippy. Hey, we'll be like wedding crashers, only a little more obvious and on a serious mission. To get the girl. And if there's a possibility of getting a slice of cake in the process, so be it."

Giovanni laughed. It's not like he wasn't tempted to try to get the wedding canceled. He liked Natalie. A lot. In fact, he was pretty sure he was falling in love with her.

She was an angel.

That kiss told him that she felt something too, but would that something be enough for her to not marry Jacks? That was the million-dollar question.

The phone rang and Giovanni checked the ID.

"It's my mom again. I'm not gonna pick up."

"I don't blame you," said Stevie. "Your mom is like a hyena."

"That's not far off target," said Danny. "Female hyenas wear the pants in the family, you know. A female hyena has a pseudopenis and—"

"Enough!" yelled Giovanni.

Stevie and Danny stared at Giovanni.

Giovanni shrugged. "Sorry. It's just…my mom is driving me crazy."

The phone rang again. Enough was enough. He was going to tell his mom to mind her own business.

He answered the call and said, "Mom. This is enough. I —"

"Hi Giovanni, it's me. James."

"James? Hi! Sorry. How are you?"

"Good. I love the guitar you gave me. The performance was good too. They threw flowers at me."

"That means they really liked you!"

"I know. Thanks again for the guitar. Can I talk with Natalie?"

"Oh. Well…she's not here. She's probably getting ready for her wedding tomorrow."

"Oh."

"You sound disappointed, James."

"I may be eight, but I notice things. I saw the way she looked at you. It was how my mom used to look at my dad.

And my mom loved my dad a lot."

"Really…"

"Yeah. A lot. Do you love Natalie?"

Giovanni let out a deep breath. Danny and Stevie were staring at him, very interested in this conversation. Too interested.

"Hold on, James," said Giovanni.

"Okay."

Giovanni covered the mouthpiece with his palm. "Can you guys wait outside for a moment?"

"Why?" asked Stevie. "You gonna get all mushy mushy?"

"Out!"

"You don't have to yell. I'm sensitive."

"Right."

The boys walked outside and closed the door behind them.

"Okay, James. I'm back. And the answer to your question is yes. I love her."

"What did she say when you told her? She loves you too, right?"

"I never told her."

"Oh. Mr. McLeod is calling me so I need to get off the phone. But I don't think you should let Natalie marry that other guy. She's very pretty. And she smells good."

Giovanni laughed. "I agree with you there. I like the way she smells too."

"I'll call you again. Is that okay?"

"Of course it's okay. Thanks for the advice. You're very wise for your age."

*****

Natalie sat at the kitchen table eating pancakes with Federico. She moaned with every bite. "These are the best, Nono. I could eat these every day. How about I just live with you forever and forget about men?"

He shook his head. "That would not be a very satisfying life. Yes, we would be able to enjoy things together but I won't be here forever. Besides, you need more."

"Like pancakes?"

He chuckled. "Yes, like pancakes. But true satisfaction of life comes from the love of someone you are intimate with. There is nothing like it in the world. I've had amazing moments in my life, but the most satisfying, the most memorable, and the most fulfilling moments were the ones I shared with Olive."

"That's sweet."

"She was an angel. And *that's* when you know you have someone special! When you believe a person is an angel."

Giovanni was *not* an angel. More like a god. Good-looking, kind, generous, compassionate, and she loved his sense of humor.

Wait. Why was she thinking of Giovanni again?

Fudge!

Not good. She was getting married tomorrow and she was thinking of another man. She needed to get her shit together and—

Federico pointed to her fork. "How long are you going to hold that bite of pancake in the air?"

Natalie stared at the fork. "Oh." She popped it in her mouth and moaned again.

"I can see that you are preoccupied with things. This is normal. They call it the pre-wedding jitters, no?"

She nodded. "I guess." She felt her eyes water.

Don't cry. Don't cry. Don't cry.

A tear hit the table. Then another.

Federico stood up and kissed her on the forehead. "Bambina. Everything is going to be okay. All you have to do is follow your heart."

She sobbed and choked out the words, "Follow my heart?"

"Yes! The heart *always* knows."

She sniffed and wiped her nose. "How do you know all of this? Are you making it up to try to make me feel better?"

He smiled. "When you're not around I read Oprah Magazine."

She laughed out loud and snorted. "I love you, Nono."

"I love you too."

She analyzed him for a moment. "Do you miss Nana?"

He smiled. "She's here with me. I can feel her in the house as I do my day-to-day things. And sometimes I hear her voice."

Natalie, now full of curiosity, put down her fork. "What does she say?"

"Don't forget to take out the garbage."

Natalie playfully smacked her grandfather on the arm. "I thought it was going to be something romantic! That is not romantic. Does she say anything else?"

He nodded. "She thanks me for making her feel loved. For treating her as if she was the only woman in the world. And for not complaining about all of her kisses."

"Who would complain about that?"

"Exactly! It's an expression of love and I could never deny her that. Besides, I loved them. They were little shots of energy in my day. Like espresso, only sweeter."

She smiled and rubbed the top of his hand.

And there went her mind again…back to Giovanni's kiss. Jacks never kissed her like that.

She sighed and pretended to clean the kitchen window. Giovanni was nowhere in sight. And why would he be? She told him to take a hike.

She went to her room and plopped on the bed, staring up at the ceiling. What was her heart telling her? She was getting mixed signals. Or maybe that was her brain trying to get involved. One thing was for sure, if she wasn't one hundred percent sure her doubts were real, she would proceed forward as planned.

She would marry Jacks.

Chapter Seventeen

This could be quite possibly the stupidest thing Giovanni had ever done in his life. Well, second if you count kissing a woman at her wedding rehearsal, of course. And let's face it, there's no way that could be overlooked.

It was Natalie's wedding day and Giovanni and the boys were rushing out the door to her wedding to stop her from marrying Jacks.

Was he insane? Yeah, probably.

And maybe he would return later without the girl and a second black eye. But the pain of that second black eye would be a thousand times less than the pain of regret. He felt anxiety pumping through his veins. He was excited, but also wanted to puke his guts out.

Stevie unlocked the doors to his Cadillac.

Danny paused and looked under the car. "I see a wet spot underneath your Caddy, Stevie. You're leaking shit."

Stevie wiped a water stain off the hood with the bottom of his shirt. "The only wet spot I will ever have in my life is the one I have to occasionally sleep in. As for the car, this is a finely-tuned, well-oiled machine. I've told you a thousand times that this baby is in cherry condition. Get in."

Giovanni looked under the car and confirmed what Danny had said. "I think Danny is right. It definitely looks like you're leaking shit."

"I ain't leaking shit!"

"Are you blind?"

"No. I am not blind, smart ass. That shit was already there."

"How do you know that shit was already there?"

"I just know, you know? It was already there. Now enough of this shit about that shit. Get in the car."

The boys got in the car and Danny turned to Stevie. "You better not be leaking shit. You know how important this day is for Giovanni? He found his balls and is going to get the girl!"

"I am telling you...I am *not* leaking shit!"

Fifteen minutes later Stevie was driving up the hill to Thousand Castles Winery. The boys were admiring the view from up above when the engine started to hesitate.

Then the engine died.

Stevie pulled his Cadillac on to the side of the road. "Nobody better not say shit about shit."

"Can I at least say something about your use of the English language?" said Danny. "It's horrific."

"No."

"That was like a double or triple negative, you know? You shouldn't do that."

Stevie gave Danny a look.

Danny threw his palms up. "What?"

Stevie popped open the hood and smoke billowed out.

Danny imitated Stevie. "This is a finely-tuned, well-oiled machine. You know this baby is in cherry condition. Blah, blah, blah, bullshit. If Giovanni doesn't get the girl it's all your fault!"

Stevie pointed to the engine. "This is just a coincidence. It has nothing to do with the wet spot on the street."

"Right."

The boys heard a car coming and all turned to watch a white van coming in their direction. The van had printing on the side that said "Eagle Bridge Bakery, Owner - Phil Jackson."

The van driver stopped in the middle of the street and rolled down his window. He was wearing a white baker's jacket with a company logo.

"Hey," said the driver.

"Hey," said Stevie.

"Hey," said Danny.

"Hey," said Giovanni.

The driver pointed to Stevie's car. "Not a good place to break down."

Stevie stared at the car. "Is there such a thing?"

"What?"

"A good place to break down?"

The driver thought for a moment and looked at the car. "How about in front of Disneyland?"

Danny nodded. "That's a pretty good place."

Stevie agreed. "Can't argue with that. Can you give us a lift?"

"I can't. I am going up to the winery for a wedding."

"Then why did you stop if you can't help us?"

The driver thought about it for a moment. He opened his mouth and then closed it.

"Forget the question," said Stevie. "We're going to the wedding too so could you please give us a lift?

The driver pointed to the van. "There are no seats in the back. Just the cake."

"No big deal. We'll squat. It's just up the hill."

"Okay."

Giovanni pointed to Stevie's car. "What about the car?"

Stevie looked back at his car. "It'll be okay here. This is a private road. I'll get it towed after the wedding. We've got more important things to worry about now. Like making sure the bride doesn't marry—"

Giovanni slapped Stevie on the arm.

The driver stared at Stevie, waiting for him to continue. He looked a little suspicious.

"…Until we get there! We don't want to miss the wedding. Let's go!"

Good recovery.

Stevie sat in the passenger seat and Danny and Giovanni jumped in the back of the van and squatted next to the cake.

Giovanni felt like an idiot, but at least it would get him

where he needed to be.

Danny leaned in toward to the cake and inhaled deeply through his nose. "What type of cake is this?"

The driver looked in the rear view mirror. "Red velvet with cream cheese frosting."

"Really." Danny eyed the cake again and took another whiff. He reached his index finger out toward the cake and Giovanni grabbed it and held on to it.

"Don't even think about it," whispered Giovanni.

"Just a touch on the finger tip," he whispered back. "They won't even notice."

"No."

They played tug of war with Danny's finger until the one thing Giovanni didn't want to happen, happened. Danny's finger slipped from his grip and flew into the side of the cake along with his entire fist. The cake now had a hole in the side of it the size of a softball.

Giovanni couldn't hold back his shock. "Son of a baracuda!"

The driver slowed the van but didn't stop it completely. He looked in the rear view mirror again and asked, "Everything okay?"

Giovanni waved to him. "Yeah, yeah. Sorry about that. It's just…I left the wedding gift at home."

"Ahhh. No big deal. The bride and groom don't usually open their gifts until they get home from their honeymoon."

"Okay. Good to know."

"Hey, what's that noise?"

That noise happened to be Danny licking the frosting off his hand like a mad man. Or more like a dog that was giving himself a bath. He was very thorough, but when he started to moan Giovanni punched him in the arm.

"Ouch!"

The driver slowed the van down again. "Now what?"

"Nothing. I just have a hangnail that's a bitch!"

Giovanni did his best to patch up the cake, but only made it look worse. They arrived at the winery at the top of the hill and it started to rain. The boys got out and thanked the driver for the lift. A large group of people ran by them into the winery.

"What's going on?" asked Giovanni.

"Looks like they moved the ceremony inside," said the driver. "They do that when it rains. There's a wine cellar they use as a backup ceremony site."

The driver moved around to the back of the van to pull the cake out.

"Quick," said Giovanni to Danny and Stevie. "Let's get inside."

Danny pointed toward the car in front of the entrance. "Nice ride!"

It was Jacks' Camaro. On display for everyone to see. Of course. On the back window of the car, it said, "Jacks & Natalie Forever."

Right.

Not if Giovanni could help it.

Stevie ran his hand along the roof of the car. "This, my friends, is a 1969 Chevrolet Camaro ZL1." He looked through the window. "And it looks like it's been restored to original factory specifications. Unbelievable. This is one of the rarest muscle cars in the world."

Giovanni shrugged. "It's nice, but still. It's just a car."

Stevie wagged his finger at Giovanni. "Maybe to you. But to the owner of this car there is nothing more important in life."

"Sounds pretty pathetic to me. Come on, let's go."

They entered the main building and passed through the tasting room to the cellar. Giovanni pointed to some empty seats and the boys followed him and sat.

Giovanni's heartbeat kicked up a notch. Jacks was at the front of the cellar near the altar talking with the pastor and his best man. Giovanni looked around the room for his mom. He could hear her words echoing in his head.

If you don't stop the wedding, I will! I want grandchildren! Do you hear me?

Would she show up? Hell yeah, she would.

The pastor spoke into the microphone. "Good evening. The ceremony is about to commence so if you could please silence your cell phones—that would be fantastic. There usually isn't any cell phone coverage here in the cellar, but just in case. Better safe than sorry. Thank you."

Giovanni checked his phone and it was already on vibrate.

And the pastor was right, no signal at all. He looked around the cellar. "These walls must be made of cement or something."

"Actually, it looks like they built this place directly into the side of the mountain," said Danny. "That would mean it's all natural and we would be completely surrounded by limestone and dolomite."

Giovanni tapped Danny on the side of the leg. "I think we should talk more about that. It helps with my nerves if I'm not thinking of the current situation and what I'm about to do."

Danny smiled. "You know I eat this stuff up. Just like cake." He inspected a finger. "Ooh, more frosting." He smiled and licked it.

"Sorry to disrupt your peace," said Stevie. "You're not going to like this."

Giovanni turned to Stevie. "Like what?"

Stevie gestured to his right where Eleonora was seated.

"Son of a biscuit," he said in a low voice.

Just what he needed, his mom interfering with things. With her present there was no telling what could happen. He had no doubts she was going to make a scene. Her balls were so big she could go bowling with them. Giovanni had to make his move first or his mother could blow everything.

Giovanni leaned toward Stevie and Danny. "Okay, here's the plan. When the pastor asks if anyone objects to the wedding I make my move. If my mom tries to make a move first, tackle her. Got it?"

Danny ran his fingers through his hair. "I don't think they ask if anyone objects to the wedding anymore. That's just in the movies."

"Then I just need to find the right place to do it. But keep in mind my mom may try to say something and I need to do it first. Got it?"

"Yeah," said Danny. "Then what? You want us to hold the groom down while you take off with the bride?"

"Of course not. You two stay out of this unless you see my mom doing something I should know about. Then tell me. I just need to focus on standing up when it's time."

"What are you going to say?"

"I haven't the slightest idea."

*****

Natalie messed around with her hair and sighed. She dropped her hair and stared closer at her face in the bathroom mirror. "No way!"

Rebecca yelled from the other room. "What?"

"I have a zit. The size of a walnut."

Rebecca rushed in and looked at her face. She adjusted her purple bridesmaid dress. "Let me see. Move your hand and look at me."

Natalie turned to Rebecca and she inspected the zit. Rebecca moved in for a closer look and touched the zit. The photographer stepped in and took a picture just as she touched it.

Rebecca squished her eyebrows together.

"Well?" asked Natalie. "How bad is it?"

"Uh..."

"That's it. The wedding is off! I'm not getting married with a crater on my face."

"Hold still!"

Rebecca licked her finger and carefully wiped the zit off. "Chocolate. You need to relax. There is no need to get nervous."

Natalie inspected her ears. "I have very large ears."

"You do not have large ears."

Natalie played with her ears and pulled them out away from her head so they looked even bigger. "Look, I'm Dumbo."

The photographer stepped up and snapped her picture as she held her ears out.

"What's wrong with me? I should be happy."

Rebecca rubbed her shoulder. "You should be."

"Something doesn't feel right."

"Did you smoke pot?"

"No."

"Maybe you should."

"I'm a cop—I'm not going to smoke pot." Natalie started crying. The photographer stepped up again and snapped another photo.

Rebecca turned toward the photographer, her hands on her hips. "Do you really think she's going to want that picture in her photo album?"

The photographer thought about it and said nothing. He stepped back and pulled another lens from his bag.

Natalie continued to cry. "I wanted a fairy-tale wedding."

"That's what you're going to have, sweetie."

"I just have this feeling that something is going to go terribly wrong. My instincts are always right."

"What are you talking about? This is a beautiful day."

"I think I hear rain and rain is bad luck."

"No, it is not raining. And you planned this day out perfectly. Nothing is going to go wrong. Let me see a smile, come on."

Natalie gave her a fake smile. "How's this?"

Rebecca wiped Natalie's eyes carefully with some tissue. "There you go. Be happy! You're getting married!"

"Yeah, I'm going to marry Jackson Cole."

"Of course you are, sweetie."

"No, you don't understand. I'm going to be Natalie Cole. Don't you see? The jokes will never stop!"

"It's just a name! You love him, right?"

"What is love?"

"Oh boy." Rebecca rolled up a napkin to make it look like a joint and pretended to take a hit of it. As she exhaled, the photographer stepped forward and snapped a picture.

Chapter Eighteen

Giovanni counted about seventy-five guests in the white chairs around him. A pianist sat at the piano to the left of the altar.

Giovanni's replacement.

He felt some guilt, but then realized this was all supposed to happen. Life was sometimes crazy and you just had to go with it.

The wedding coordinator gave the pianist the cue to start the music.

The pianist played Pachelbel's 'Canon in D'.

"This song won't go away," said Stevie. He turned to Danny and held up his finger. "Listen to me very carefully. If you mention one word about this song or this artist or how his music was forgotten or anything that has to do with music, songs, instruments, ensembles, operas, conductors, symphonies, compositions, orchestras, choirs, concerts, notes, lyrics, MP3s, or musicians, I will stick my foot so far up your ass you'll be able to floss your teeth with my shoelaces."

"I wasn't going to say anything!"

"Right."

Giovanni stared at Jacks who swayed back and forth to the

music as he stood next to the pastor. He didn't blame the guy for punching him, but Natalie deserved better.

I want it to be me.

The bridesmaids walked the aisle, followed by Rebecca, the matron of honor. Then Natalie appeared and began to walk down the aisle, escorted by her grandfather Federico.

She was absolutely beautiful. An angel. The only thing that could have made her more attractive would have been a smile on her lips. She obviously was not happy. All the more reason to say something when the opportunity came up. She didn't see Giovanni, which was probably good.

Federico was a different story. He winked at Giovanni and continued up the aisle with his granddaughter.

When Natalie arrived at the altar the pastor said, "Who gives this woman to be married?"

"I do," said Federico.

"Thank you. You may be seated."

Federico kissed his granddaughter and took a seat in the front row. Natalie stepped up and stood next to Jacks.

"I'd first like to welcome you all to this very special occasion," said the pastor. "To celebrate the love of Natalie and Jack."

Jacks leaned in and whispered something to the pastor.

The pastor smiled and nodded. "To celebrate the love of Natalie and...*Jacks*."

"Is there an echo in here?" asked Danny.

"What love is the pastor talking about?" whispered Stevie.

"I don't see any love."

Stevie was shushed by a woman sitting behind him.

"I'm Pastor Peter Paul Packard and I'm pleased as punch to partake in this particularly…" The pastor dropped his notes and lost his place.

Stevie leaned into Giovanni. "Peter Piper picked a peck of __"

"Not now," said Giovanni.

The pastor picked up his notes and shuffled through them. "Sorry." He tried to organize them and finally gave up. "I'm honored and it's a…celebration of…you know…different cultures…coming together. A celebration of…uh…a celebration of love!"

Stevie tapped Giovanni on the arm. "I think the pastor is high on crack or something."

The pastor adjusted his glasses, took a deep breath, and continued. "Love is the most magical, precious thing on earth. It's what drives us and keeps us going. Without love…we are nothing. Zip. Nada. A big goose egg. Love is like a peach. A *juicy* peach. You just wanna bite into it and suck the juice all day long."

"A peach sounds peachy," said Danny.

"So before we officially begin the ceremony…if there is anyone who feels that this marriage is not just, speak now or forever hold your peach."

The guests laughed.

The pastor turned red. "Peace. Hold your peace."

This was it, Giovanni's cue. It was now or never. Both Danny and Stevie looked at Giovanni and waited. Stevie gave Giovanni a nudge with his arm. "Showtime. Do it now before your mother does."

Giovanni stood up.

Then Eleonora stood up.

Son of a biscuit!

Before either one could speak a male voice barked out from behind them.

"Can I do both?" yelled the man in the back of the room. The guests were startled and everyone turned around. A man dressed in black stood in the back with a gun in his hand. He was accompanied by another man also dressed in black.

"Pardon me?" asked Pastor Peter Paul Packard.

The mysterious man walked up the aisle and left his goon in the back to guard the only exit. "I would like to speak now *and* as you can see, I'm holding my piece!"

The man waved his gun in the air. He started walking toward the altar. Several people dropped to the floor to hide while a few others took out their cell phones, obviously to call the police—even though there was no cell signal in the cellar.

A woman fanning herself with a Japanese fan jumped up, screamed, and pointed. "Oh my God, he's got a gun!"

"Shut up!" said the man. "Who are you, the play-by-play announcer?"

She sat back down.

The man mimicked the lady with the fan. "Oh my God! He's got a gun! And he's walking towards the bride and groom with his gun. Bang!"

The woman screamed and covered her mouth with her hand.

The gunman laughed and eyed Eleonora, who was still standing. "Who are you?"

"My name is Eleonora Roma."

The man smiled. "Nice name, Eleonora. But what do you think you're doing?"

She held her head up high and proud. If she was afraid of the gun it didn't show. "I also object to this wedding."

"Oh, do you?"

Giovanni decided to join in the conversation. "I objected first."

The man turned to Giovanni. "And who the hell are you?"

"I'm her son."

The man looked back to Eleonora. "*Her* son?"

"That's right."

"Well, I appreciate this whole family affair thing you've got going, but in case you haven't noticed I have a gun, so my objection is more important than your objections. So sit your asses down!"

Giovanni and Eleonora sat down.

The pastor chewed on one of his fingernails. "Is...there a problem?"

"Yeah, there's a problem. These two are not getting

married."

Natalie and Jacks stood there in silence. Natalie's eyes were darting back and forth between a couple of guys toward the front. Maybe they were other cops in her force and she was trying to analyze the situation and come up with a plan to do something about the intruder.

"Holy shit," said Stevie. "This is going to be good. Wish I had some popcorn."

Danny tapped on Giovanni's leg. "You gonna say anything else?"

Giovanni nodded. "I've come this far. What have I got to lose?"

"Not much. Just your life."

The pastor folded his notes and placed them in his jacket pocket. "This is usually not the way things are done when you object to a wedding. Oh, who am I kidding?" He let out a nervous laugh. "This has never happened to me before so I really don't know the rules at all. Can you put the gun away, though? It's making me nervous."

"No can do, Mr. Magoo."

"Okay then. You want to object to this marriage?"

"Yes, I most definitely do."

Giovanni stood up. "So do I!"

Giovanni worked his way from his row and walked down the aisle toward Natalie.

The man pointed the gun at him. "Didn't I tell you to sit down?"

Giovanni stopped. "Yes, you did but your request is unacceptable."

"Unacceptable? It's not a negotiation."

"Ignore him," said Jacks, pointing at Giovanni. "He's just a jackass who has the hots for my fiancée."

Giovanni met Natalie's gaze and she didn't seem to look mad that he was doing this. That was a good sign. He looked back to Jacks. "Did you not notice there's a man with a gun?"

"I know why he's here. His name is Paolo DeManera and I just helped put his brother away for life in prison. He's here because of me. You, on the other hand, have no reason to be here. You're just a jackass."

"Hey!" said Eleonora. She stood and scooted toward the aisle. "If anyone is going to call my son a jackass it's going to be me!"

"Jesus Christ," said Jacks. "Why are you objecting to this wedding anyway?"

"Because that woman standing next to you is fertile and I want her to make babies with my son! I want grandchildren, goddammit!"

Here we go again, thought Giovanni.

A man in the second row burst out in laughter.

"Hey!" Paolo pointed his gun at the man. "You think it's right to laugh at someone who is hurting? Can't you see she is going through some shit right now?"

The man stopped his laughter. "You're right. I don't know

what I was thinking. I should be ashamed of myself. I apologize."

Paolo stared at the guy. "Are you serious? That didn't sound sincere at all. I think you're just saying that so I don't shoot you."

"You're right, that's exactly why I said it. I don't want to be shot. I'm sorry. I don't know what I was thinking."

"You sound like a fucking robot! Knock it off unless you are going to give me some sincerity."

"I'll work on that. I'm sorry. I—"

"I'm warning you!"

The man closed his mouth.

"What's your name?"

The man ran his fingers through his hair. "Justin."

"You got sisters, Justin?"

"No."

"Of course not. That's why you don't know about women and their emotions. You don't know what they go through. You got a girlfriend?"

Justin smiled and sat up higher. "Yeah."

"Okay, now we're getting somewhere. What's her name?"

Justin looked around the room as if it was a trick question. He didn't answer.

"I asked you a question. What's her name?"

"Star."

"Your girlfriend's name is Star?

"Yeah."

"Like star in the sky? Star?"

"Yes."

"I used to have a horse named Star."

"Okay…"

"She's dead. I shot her, but that's another story. So tell me, where does Star work?"

The man shrugged. "Nowhere if she's dead."

"Not my horse you idiot, your girlfriend!"

Justin grimaced. "Oh. Sorry."

"Knock off the 'sorrys' and answer the question!"

"She's manager at Hot Dog On A Stick."

"Very impressive. Sounds like marriage material. Anyway, let's say *Star* comes home from Hot Dog on a Stick and is having a *very* bad day. Maybe she pitched the CEO an idea about expanding the menu so they offered hamburger on a stick. Then her idea gets shot down. She's not going to be a happy camper at all, Justin. You gonna laugh at her?"

He looked at Paolo like he was crazy. "Why would I do that? Hamburger on a stick sounds like an awesome idea."

A man next to Justin nodded and said, "That *does* sound pretty good. Someone should invent that—I would eat there."

Paolo sighed. "Hey genius, the Persians invented it about a billion years ago. It's called the fucking kebab. Stay with me here. My point is not about that. I'm asking you if you would laugh at Star if she was sad or having a terrible day."

Justin thought about it for a few seconds. "No. I wouldn't."

Paolo scratched the side of his face with the gun. "Of course you wouldn't! Now *this* woman is having a bad day. What gives you the right to laugh at her? Put yourself in her shoes. How do you think she feels? I want you to feel her pain. Be compassionate and have a little respect."

Eleonora nodded. "Thank you."

"It's the least I can do."

Justin opened his mouth and then closed it.

"What?" asked Paolo. "You were going to say something? Say it."

Justin shrugged. "It's just that you're talking about respect and all, but you just crashed a wedding with a gun. That's not very respectful at all, is it?"

Paolo nodded and paced back and forth. "Not respectful at all. You've got a good point there. You're right—it's *not* respectful at all." He paced a few more times. "But I don't give a shit! Having a gun allows a person certain *liberties*, you know what I'm saying?" He spun the gun around on one finger and some of the guests ducked down in their seats. The gun stopped spinning on his finger and he winced and bit his fingernail. "Damn! Anyone got a fingernail clipper?"

What kind of mafia guy was this? He was going to do some grooming now?

"I do!" said the wedding coordinator. She ran up to the front with her little bag of goodies and sat it on top of the piano. She shuffled through some things inside of the bag and handed him the nail clippers.

"Thank you." He clipped part of his fingernail and dropped it on the floor. "Now, where was I? Oh, yeah, I was going to kill the bride."

Federico stood up. "That is probably not a good idea."

"Yeah? Why not, old man?"

"She's a cop."

Paolo yanked his head around to Natalie and checked her out from head to toe. "I don't see it."

"Believe me, she is. And one of the best cops in the city, I might add. And it may also be helpful to know that there are two other cops in this room and at least ten lawyers."

Paolo scanned the room. "Seriously? Shit. Of course I knew about the lawyers, but I had no clue about the cops. I'm new at this and still learning the ropes." He looked to the back of the room where the other guy was guarding the door. "My partner did not do his homework very well either, did he?"

The guy shrugged.

Giovanni fidgeted in his seat and wanted to say something. He could see Natalie looking around the room for something. Was she sending signals to the other cops? Maybe she had a plan to stop the guy. She could always just kick him in the shins.

Paolo handed the fingernail clippers back to the wedding coordinator. "I guess it doesn't matter if she's a cop, really." He pointed to Jacks. "This man sent my brother away for life and tore apart my family. So...*you* need to suffer for it. I thought about killing you, but then that's not suffering at all! That's when I came up with the idea of killing your bride. That will make you suffer."

Jacks shrugged. "Fine. I'm going to suffer, you're right." He pushed Natalie at Paolo. "Go ahead. Kill her."

What a jerk.

Giovanni stood up. "Wait!" He moved to the front and became a shield in between Paolo and Natalie.

Paolo let out a deep breath. "You again? You're like a bad case of something that not even penicillin can get rid of. What do you want this time?"

"Don't kill her. Kill me."

Chapter Nineteen

Natalie couldn't believe what she was hearing. Giovanni was willing to die for her. God, that made him even sexier. If that was possible.

She glanced over at the man she was supposed to marry. Jacks did nothing—didn't even say anything to defend or protect her. She had decided to go through with the wedding —she had felt guilty about breaking it off and hurting him. Then Jacks threw her to the lions.

Talk about one hundred percent betrayal.

Paolo pointed the gun at Giovanni. "What are you doing?"

"If you're going to kill someone, kill *me.*"

"Yeah, great idea," said Jacks. "Kill him."

Paolo stared at Giovanni for a moment. "I'm not going to kill you! I don't even *know* you! And how is that going to hurt him, anyway? Sit down!"

Giovanni pointed to Natalie. "Killing her is not going to hurt him either! He doesn't care about her!"

"And you do?"

Giovanni nodded. "Yes—absolutely. In fact, I love her. It's crazy because we just met, but I do. And I can't bear the thought of anything happening to her. So if you're dead set on killing her, kill me too."

There were a few audible "awws" in the crowd.

"Interesting development here." Paolo paced back and forth. "I'll be honest—I'm not sure what to do. I'm new at this gangster stuff, you know?" Paolo analyzed Giovanni and pointed to his face with the gun. "How did you get the black eye?"

"From the guy standing next to you."

Paolo turned to Jacks. "You did that?"

Jacks nodded proudly.

Eleonora stormed to the front and got in Jacks' face. "How dare you do that to my son!"

"He kissed my fiancée."

"I don't care if he bent her over the dining room table." She wound up and punched Jacks in the face.

Jacks covered his nose with his hand and screamed. "You crazy bitch!"

Natalie tried to hold in a smile. Giovanni's mom wasn't so bad after all. Obsessed with grandchildren, yes. But she still cared about her son. Natalie glanced over at Giovanni, who was staring at her. Yeah, she had feelings for him.

Strong feelings.

And showing up today to marry Jacks was a mistake. What was she thinking? She didn't want to hurt Jacks' feelings, but that wasn't a good enough reason to marry someone.

Paolo eyed Eleonora. "You single?"

"Afraid not."

"Too bad." His eyes dropped down to her chest, then rose back up to connect with her eyes. "Did you really come here to stop the wedding because you want your son to bang the bride?"

"As I said before she's very fertile."

Federico stood and held up his index finger. "Excuse me."

Paolo sighed. "What do you want, Grandpa? You going to object to the wedding too? Join the club."

"I don't object, but I don't agree with it either. It's not my business to tell my granddaughter what to do. I just want her to be happy and as I told her yesterday, she needs to follow her heart."

Paolo nodded. "Good advice. Why you standing up then? The diaper's all full?"

"I wanted to tell a story."

"Right now?"

"Yes."

Paolo studied Federico and then nodded. "Okay." He hopped up on top of the piano and gestured to him. "Be my guest."

"Thank you." Federico stood there thinking, possibly trying to gather his thoughts.

What was he up to? Natalie was getting tired of standing and doing nothing. She would have tried to do something, tried to apprehend Paolo, but her dress was keeping her from doing almost anything at all. She could barely move. It was the most uncomfortable dress she had ever worn, and truth be told, she didn't even like it very much. It wasn't her first choice, but Jacks insisted she wear his grandmother's wedding dress from the fifties. It took two cleanings just to remove the smell of mothballs.

Federico looked around at the many guests who were staring at him. They had his full attention. "It was 1940 when I met Olive at a carnival. She was the most beautiful woman in the world and we were set to have a summer love affair of a lifetime. It was love at first sight, I tell you. The only thing I wanted to do was spend every waking minute with her, romance her, and make her mine. Nothing mattered more to me. Nothing. I recited poetry from Walt Whitman to her every chance I got and her eyes would sparkle with each poem."

Paolo nodded. "I tried reciting the words to "Baby Got Back" one time." He grimaced. "It didn't work so well." He cleared his throat. "Sorry. Please continue—I'm really enjoying the story."

"Thank you. Olive and I grew closer and closer to each other, but little did we know that a force stronger than our love was trying to keep us apart." Federico poked himself in the chest with his index finger. "I was a boy from the wrong side of the tracks and her mother could not bear that. So she banned her daughter from seeing me. She said I was trash."

Natalie looked around the room. Some of the guests wiped their eyes, even a few of the men. She turned and looked at Paolo. He sat on the piano, crying like a big baby.

Paolo wiped his eyes and sniffled. "I hope this has a happy ending."

Federico nodded and continued. "It wasn't long after that when her mother took the family and moved away. I was devastated and convinced they moved away because of me. I would later find out it was the truth. I wrote letters to her every single day for a year, but never received a single response. I also found out her mother was hiding the letters so her daughter could not see them. What kind of a person would do such a thing?"

Paolo wiped his eyes. "A bitch! That's who!"

"Heartbroken, I enlisted to fight in World War II and after that I—"

"Wait a minute, wait a minute, wait a goddamn minute," said Paolo. He jumped off the piano and wiped his eyes. He blew his nose and then rolled up the tissue into a ball and stuck it in his pocket.

Inching closer to Federico, he wagged his finger in front of his face. "This little love story of yours sounds a little bit fishy, Grandpa."

"I'm not sure what you mean."

"I mean the story, *this* story…it sounds familiar. I just can't put my finger on it at the moment."

"I think you are mistaken."

"Got it! You sneaky son of a bitch. That's from a Nicholas Sparks movie, I'm sure of it. He scratched his chin with the gun. "*The Notebook!* That's it! Jesus Christ. My second ex-wife made me watch that movie so many times. On our anniversary. On Valentine's Day. Always when she had PMS. *The Notebook.* Don't you deny it!"

Federico nodded. "It's common knowledge that people my age tend to blend fiction with reality and many times can't tell the two apart. My doctor told me he saw the warning signs. Thank you for catching that—I will report the results to my doctor."

Federico sat down and folded his hands in his lap. Natalie tried to hold back the laughter. She had no idea what he was trying to accomplish by telling that story, but it was entertaining at least.

Paolo cleared his throat and stuck his chest out. "Enough of these shenanigans—change of plans again. I gotta shoot someone. I guess I'll just shoot the groom. "

"Stop!" said Giovanni.

Paolo cocked his head to the side. "Again? You love the groom too?"

"No!" Giovanni let out a deep breath. "Paolo, right?"

"Yeah."

"Look Paolo, killing him won't solve anything either. It's unfortunate, but you got tossed into a situation you don't want to be in, right?"

"That's right."

"You seem like a nice guy, I can see that. Sensitive. Passionate."

Paolo blushed. "Thank you. I often wondered if people noticed those qualities in me."

"For sure! I noticed immediately. Now listen…if you kill him, you would be sharing a jail cell with your brother. Do you want to spend the rest of your life in jail? Because killing Jacks is not worth it."

"I can appreciate where you're coming from and agree with you, but I gotta do *something*. What happened to my brother was a disgrace to the family and now the pressure is on me to take over and rebuild our reputation."

"I have a solution!" yelled Stevie, making his way to the front.

"Jesus Christ," said Paolo. "Another one?" He points the gun at Stevie. "Please state your name and your solution and make it fast."

"My name is Stevie Marino. I'm a Sagittarius." He points to Giovanni. "And I'm best friends with this very kind man. He's right, killing that douchebag wouldn't solve anything. If you want to make this man pay, you need to hit him where it hurts the most."

Paolo pointed the gun at Jacks' crotch. "In the balls?"

"No. Not a bad choice at all though, but no. His most prized possession is the Camaro sitting right outside."

"Is that right?"

"Yup. That's not your average Camaro from the sixties. In fact, there are only sixty-nine of them in the entire world. Now I'm not telling you to do anything to his car—I don't want to get in trouble, okay? I'm just *saying*...his car is outside and he values it more than anything else in the world, including the bride. You can use that information however you see fit. That's all I have to say on the matter."

Paolo smiled.

"Don't you even think about it," said Jacks.

"Don't worry!" said Paolo. "I'm not going to do a thing. Am I, Bruno?"

Paolo winked at his partner at the other end of the cellar. Bruno shrugged.

Paolo sighed. "I repeat...*I* am not going to do anything to his Camaro."

"Oh!" said Bruno. He disappeared out the door. A few seconds later gunshots rang out. Twelve. Maybe fifteen. Bruno returned and gave Paolo a thumbs-up.

"Noooooooooo!" said Jacks. He pushed Natalie out of the way and grabbed Paolo's arm, knocking the gun out from his hand. The gun discharged when it hit the floor.

Both Eleonora and Natalie fell.

"I've been hit!" yelled Eleonora. "I've been hit, goddammit!"

Natalie jumped up and grabbed Paolo's wrist with both of her hands and twisted it sideways and upward behind his back. Then she pushed him up against one of the wine barrels along the wall.

Paolo screamed in pain. "Uncle! Uncle!"

Stevie dove for the gun and popped back up on his feet.

271

"Go ahead. Make my day."

"Give me the gun," said a man who stepped up quickly. One of Natalie's coworkers on the force.

Stevie frowned and handed him the gun. The man went after Bruno, who slipped out the door again.

Giovanni rushed to Natalie and grabbed Paolo's other arm. "Fancy meeting you here."

"Take off your tie," said Natalie.

Giovanni grinned. "Shouldn't we wait until we get to a place with more privacy?"

"When was the last time I kicked you in the shins?"

"That's all you needed to say."

"She's a tough girl," said Paolo. "I can see why you like her. Reminds me of my third wife."

Giovanni took off his tie and handed it to Natalie. She grabbed Paolo's other wrist and twisted his arm back so that his hands were aligned. Just like that, they were tied together.

"Stay," she said.

Giovanni just stared at Natalie with a big grin on his face.

She pointed a finger at him. "Quit looking at me like that. You jinxed my wedding."

"I'm pretty sure it was doomed from the start. I have a lot of experience to back up my observation. Plus, I can't help looking at you like that. Have you seen yourself?"

"I try not to look at myself while I'm getting married."

"You're beautiful and I love—"

"Hellooooo?" yelled Eleonora.

Most of the wedding guests were on their feet now, talking, and snapping photos of Eleonora with their smartphones.

"I'm dying over here!" screamed Eleonora. "A slow death. And what does my only son do while I'm dying? He flirts with the baby maker instead of saying his final goodbye to the woman who brought him into this world. The woman who had a twenty hour labor with him. Something's wrong with this picture, people!"

Giovanni turned and gazed down to the floor where his mother laid, a handful of people around her. Someone was actually petting her head.

"Stop that!" said Eleonora, swatting the woman's hand away. "You think that comforts me? I am not a dog! And do you know how much I paid to have my hair done yesterday? I would guess more than your weekly salary!"

The kind woman got up, lowered her head, and slowly walked away. Giovanni moved toward his mother and knelt beside her. One of her hands was wrapped in a handkerchief and he could see blood.

"I'm dying, son. Do you care? I think not. Woe is me. Woe. Is. Me."

He unwrapped the handkerchief on her hand. The fingernail on her pinkie was gone. That was it.

Eleonora gasped for air. "Say goodbye to your father for me. Tell him I love him after all."

Natalie leaned down and placed her hand on Eleonora's arm to comfort her. "You're going to be okay."

"I'm not sure about that. What is your name again?"

"Natalie."

"I'm sorry, Natalie, for pressuring you to bang my son. If you knew the whole story you'd understand. I was an only child, just like Giovanni. Did you know that?"

"No. I didn't."

"Of course you didn't. We don't know each other well enough and there's no time for it now. It would have been nice to get together for tea or coffee or a couple of sweet shots of Amaretto. Oh, how I love it Amaretto…the heat as it goes down. Anyway, where was I?"

"You were an only child."

"Right! After I had Giovanni the doctor told me I would never be able to have children again. Giovanni was my only child and my only hope for grandchildren. All of my friends have grandchildren and I get so jealous. I want what they have. Do you understand? Do you see why I may have been a tiny bit obsessed with having grandchildren?"

Giovanni sighed. "A *tiny* bit?"

Eleonora ignored Giovanni's comment. "But now that I'm going to die, you can do whatever you want since I won't be here to see it. You don't have to bang him if you don't want to."

"I'll keep that in mind." Natalie pointed to her hand. "Let me see the wound."

Giovanni unwrapped her hand again and Natalie leaned in to look at it.

Natalie snorted.

"I can't believe you're laughing at me. I'm dying! I've been shot! Oh dear God. The room seems to be spinning a little bit. I think my time is near. Don't cry for me, Argentina!"

"Mom, you're missing a fingernail, not a limb."

"Seriously?" Eleonora held her head up and inspected her hand. Then she flipped it over and checked out the other side. "How is that possible? Because it hurts like a son of a bitch." She sat up, pointed at Natalie with her good hand, and smiled. "Okay, good news then. You and I are *back* in business. Eight kids. That's all I'm asking for. You two need to get busy."

"Mom!"

"I'm joking!"

One of Natalie's other coworkers grabbed Paolo and escorted him toward the exit.

Jacks approached, a bloody tissue stuffed inside one of his nostrils. "Obviously this isn't going to work out." He held out his hand to Natalie. "The ring, please."

Eleonora sighed. "Do you know how tacky that is?"

"It's none of your business."

Natalie handed Jacks the ring. Eleonora swung her leg around and knocked Jacks' legs out from under him. He hit the ground hard and screamed like a girl.

"Shut up," said Eleonora. "You big pussy."

Chapter Twenty

A week later Giovanni and Natalie held hands as they approached the entrance of the dog park with Precious. They'd seen each other every day since Natalie's almost-wedding. Giovanni was right; they had an amazing connection. He'd never met anyone like her and was so excited to spend every possible moment with her.

And kiss her. No way he was going to forget that.

He'd met a lot of women in his life, but he was positive that Natalie was *the one.* They agreed to take it slow, but Giovanni really wasn't too sure how long he could wait before popping the question. It was crazy, but this was real. He felt it.

He smiled, opened the first gate, and they stepped inside with the energetic dog.

"Arf!"

"Someone's excited," said Giovanni.

He pushed open the second gate and undid the leash. Precious bolted toward her labradoodle friend. Giovanni and Natalie sat on the same bench as before and watched as the dogs played and ran in all different directions. They continued to hold hands.

Giovanni smiled as the pug from last week walked in their direction. "Here comes reincarnated Hairy."

Natalie laughed and stuck out her hand as the pug approached. The dog licked her hand and she scratched it on the head. "I don't think he would come back as a pug."

"I think it's him. This dog is attached to you. Like me."

"You're not going to lick my hand, are you?"

"Well, not *that* hand."

Giovanni's phone rang and he held up an index finger. "Excuse me for a moment. I'm expecting a call from a client about their guitar delivery. I'll make it quick."

She smiled. "Take your time."

He answered the call. "This is Giovanni."

"Giovanni! This is Beatrice—how is my baby?"

"Are you talking about me or the dog?"

"Ha! Good one, but I am talking about the dog."

Giovanni wasn't ready to give up Precious, but he knew this was supposed be temporary. How would he know he would get so attached to the dog?

"Precious is fine," he said. "How was your trip? Are you back in town?"

"Not quite. The trip is going very well. Okay, I might be understating things. It's the trip of a lifetime! That's why I'm calling. I'm going to extend the trip three months."

"Three more months?" Giovanni mouthed "Oh my God!" to Natalie.

It was the best news. Beatrice could never come back and

he would be perfectly fine with that. Things just kept getting better and better.

"Who am I kidding?" said Beatrice. "There's a chance I may never come back."

And better.

Giovanni smiled and squeezed Natalie's hand tighter. Just the thought of spending more time with Precious put a smile on his face.

Beatrice sighed. "By the way, I met a younger man who loves to kiss on the mouth. Unlike you!"

Giovanni laughed. "Yes, kissing on the mouth is important, but with the right person." He nodded at Natalie and pointed at her lips and she laughed. "In fact I see a beautiful pair of lips I would love to kiss at this very moment."

Natalie lost her smile and her gaze dropped to Giovanni's mouth. That look was enough for him to hang up on Beatrice. "I have to go, Beatrice. Take as long as you need. Precious is in good hands."

"That's wonderful, Giovanni, because—"

Giovanni disconnected the call and slid the phone in his pocket. He eyed Natalie's lips and then moved in slowly toward her. She closed her eyes and he was just about at the point of contact when he pulled back.

She opened her eyes—the look of disappointment all over her face. "What?"

"I just want to make sure I'm not going to get slapped

after I do this."

"I promise."

"And you're not drunk or anything, are you? I want you to remember this too."

Natalie slapped him on the arm. "I've been with you the whole day and I haven't had a single drink. Are you going to kiss me this year?"

"The forecast calls for mostly sunny skies and a ninety-nine percent chance of kisses."

"Is this your foreplay?"

"Let's just say I'm taking my time and doing it right. I want to make sure you really want this."

"I really want this."

"I don't want to take advantage of you."

"Oh God. I really think I'm going to kill you."

"I mean, I know you would take advantage of *me* and actually did on that drunken and stormy night."

She sat there quietly.

"You have nothing to say for yourself?"

"Yes, I do. First of all, it was *not* stormy that night. There were a billion stars in the sky."

"So poetic."

"Thank you. And number two, would you just shut up and kiss me before I taser you?"

"As you wish."

Giovanni leaned in and kissed her good. She moaned and squeezed his hand.

Natalie pulled away from the kiss and smiled. "Do it again."

"Incoming!"

He kissed her again.

She smiled. "Nice. Now before you go off on some verbal rampage, I want one more."

"So demanding."

Giovanni kissed her again

He felt something wet in his hand and broke off the kiss. "If that was you licking my hand, you are very talented."

They looked down and laughed when they saw Precious staring up at them.

Natalie stroked Precious, deep in thought. "Life is weird."

"How so?"

"A week ago I was supposed to get married and three weeks ago *you* were supposed to get married. Instead we're here with each other and this cute little dog. Holding hands. Kissing. No plans at all."

Giovanni grinned. "That's where you're wrong because I've got some *serious* plans for you."

Natalie smiled and pointed to a cocker spaniel. "Just like that dog over there, I'm all ears. Tell me about these plans."

"It would be a pleasure. For starters, we'll be seeing *a lot* of each other."

Natalie nodded. "That's a great start—I like that."

"Good! *And* I will be treating you like a princess, if you don't mind."

"I don't mind that at all either. Go on—you're doing really well so far."

"We need to start kissing hourly. In fact, I would like to glue my lips to yours."

Natalie laughed. "I'm okay with that too. Anything else?"

"I'm so glad you asked! We're going to come back here many more times in the future. Maybe even one day towing along an extra person."

"Your mother?"

Giovanni laughed. "No—not my mother." He cleared his throat. "Someone...*much* younger."

Natalie blushed and squeezed his hand. "Oh..."

"First we'll need to make things official, of course."

Her face beamed. "Of course."

Giovanni smiled and stared at the most beautiful woman in the world. This felt so good. So right. Still. There was just one more thing he needed to hear from her.

He held up his index finger. "But you need to promise me something."

She perked up and swallowed hard. "Anything."

"That you'll show up."

And with that, Giovanni leaned in slowly and lingered in front of her face for a few seconds. He grinned and kissed her on the lips.

Natalie pulled away—her eyes sparkling. "You keep kissing and smiling at me that way and I can guarantee I'll be there."

New Release Alert

**GET UPDATES ON
NEW RELEASES & EXCLUSIVE DEALS!**
Sign up for Rich's newsletter at:
http://www.richamooi.com/newsletter

A Note From Rich

Dear Reader,

I'm honored that you took the time to read my second novel, *Dog Day Wedding*. I hope you enjoyed the fun, crazy story of Giovanni and Natalie. I had a lot of fun writing it!

I would be so grateful if you would take the time to leave a review online at Amazon and Goodreads. It would mean the world to me and would also help new readers find my stories.

And feel free to send me an email to say hello! I love to hear from my readers—it motivates me and helps me write faster. :) My email address is rich@richamooi.com.

All the best,

Rich

Acknowledgements

It takes more than a few people to publish a book so I want to send out a big THANK YOU to everyone who helped make *Dog Day Wedding* possible.

To my very talented cover artist, Sue Traynor. Thank you for drawing another beautiful cover for me!

To Mary Yakovets for editing. Thanks so much!

A big smoochy, mushy, huggy, kissy thank you to my wife, Silvi. I'm grateful for having such an amazing person in my life that loves me and supports me and believes in what I do. Thank you for your constant help and feedback. YOU ROCK!

To romance author, Deb Julienne, for always being so helpful and kind. And to Hannah Jayne! Thanks for brainstorming with me at the very beginning.

To Robert Roffey, Isabel Anievas, Krasimir Sofijski, Kamlapati Khalsa, and Julita Sofijski. Thank you for your friendship, your support, and your help.

To Debra Holland, Sever Bronny, Chris Fox, Myra Scott, and J Gordon Smith for your input.

35670880R10179

Made in the USA
San Bernardino, CA
30 June 2016